IT WASN'T FEAR.
THE INSTINCT WAS FAR
MORE PRIMITIVE.

Kate was afraid of the feeling this man's touch might evoke within her. But she found herself rooted to the spot, his hypnotic eyes melting her helplessly with its molten gaze. He crooned softly to her, touching her with a heartbreakingly gentle caress. "Trust me, Kate."

Trust him? Trust a man who'd literally smashed his way into her home? But Kate's mind was rapidly becoming intoxicated by the glowing amber eyes, the tantalizing caresses, and Hunter's decidedly male scent. His gaze moved over her uplifted face and flames sparked within her, as his kisses claimed her with violent intensity. With the turbulence of a bursting dam, Kate's own desire flared wildly. Her mouth opened, no longer in protest, but in hot invitation....

JOANN ROBB is an incurable optimist, believing steadfastly in happy endings. She lives in Arizona with her husband and her teenage son, both of whom she fell in love with at first sight. She loves anything to do with flying, the desert, sunshine, and yellow flowers. She is the author of another Rapture Romance, *Stardust and Diamonds*.

Dear Reader:

The editors of Rapture Romance have only one thing to say—thank you! Your response to our authors, both the newcomers and the established favorites, has been enthusiastic and loyal, and we, who love our books, appreciate it.

We are committed to bringing you romances after your own heart, with the tender sensuality you've asked for and the quality you deserve. We hope that you will continue to enjoy all six Rapture Romances each month as much as we enjoy bringing them to you.

To tell you about upcoming books, introduce you to the authors, and give you an inside look at the world of Rapture Romance, we have started a free monthly newsletter. Just write to *The Rapture Reader* at the address shown below, and we will be happy to send you each issue.

And please keep writing to us! Your comments and letters have already helped us to bring you better and better books—the kind *you* want—and we depend on them. Of course, our authors also eagerly await your letters. While we can't give out their addresses, we are happy to forward any mail—writers need to hear from their fans!

Happy reading!

> Robin Grunder, Editor
> Rapture Romance
> New American Library
> 1633 Broadway
> New York, NY 10019

DREAMLOVER
by
JoAnn Robb

RAPTURE ROMANCE
NEW AMERICAN LIBRARY

PUBLISHER'S NOTE

This novel is a work of fiction. Names, characters, places, and incidents either are the product of the author's imagination or are used fictitiously, and any resemblance to actual persons, living or dead, events, or locales is entirely coincidental.

NAL BOOKS ARE AVAILABLE AT QUANTITY DISCOUNTS
WHEN USED TO PROMOTE PRODUCTS OR SERVICES.
FOR INFORMATION PLEASE WRITE TO PREMIUM MARKETING DIVISION,
THE NEW AMERICAN LIBRARY, INC., 1633 BROADWAY,
NEW YORK, NEW YORK 10019.

Copyright © 1983 by JoAnn Robb

All rights reserved

SIGNET, SIGNET CLASSIC, MENTOR, PLUME, MERIDIAN AND NAL BOOKS
are published by The New American Library, Inc.,
1633 Broadway, New York, New York 10019

First Printing, January, 1984

1 2 3 4 5 6 7 8 9

PRINTED IN THE UNITED STATES OF AMERICA

*With gratitude to Terry Mills,
for her friendship and enthusiastic support,
and Mary Anne Wilson, for her guidance
as well as her sharp pencil.*

Chapter One

She would tell herself later that she should have seen it coming; anyone with any brains at all would've immediately realized the entire scheme was riddled with flaws. The first and foremost flaw was that when you made a deal with the devil, you weren't very likely to emerge with your soul intact. Katherine Lorene Michaels would tell herself that over and over, finding little comfort in the fact that she hadn't been presented with a myriad of choices at the time.

It started innocently enough when she stopped at the post office to pick up the mail that had accumulated during her two-week absence. Reining in the urge to examine the stack of envelopes, Katherine spent the socially required length of time discussing the weather, the postmistress's grandchildren, and the influx of snowbirds to the small Arizona town.

"I swear, there's more of 'em come every season." The iron-gray head bobbed up and down as the elderly woman confirmed her own statement. "It's getting so a body can't even walk down the street without bumping smack into 'em. Used to be the cities got them all. Phoenix, Tucson. But now, they're spreading out. Mark my words, Katherine, pretty soon there'll be more of 'em around these parts than us."

Katherine had heard Mrs Drake's dissertation on the snowbirds before. Not actually referring to birds of the feathered variety, the term defined those refugees from northern climes who wintered in the sunny southwest desert. They usually arrived just before the first snows blanketed the ground back home, reaching Arizona with the migrating robins and mallards. Then, as the mercury began creeping toward the one-hundred-degree mark in the spring, they'd take wing and return home, leaving behind smiling, happy merchants.

Some of the longtime residents had never grown fond of the human migration. Katherine had heard more than one old-timer state that you could tell it was autumn in Arizona when the license plates began to change color.

Speak of the devil! Her attention wandered from Mrs Drake's increasingly strident denunciation to the tall, lean man lounging against the wall of post-office boxes. He was definitely not from around here! Katherine's alert brown eyes took in the trim lines of the Italian suit, light charcoal gray with a subdued pinstripe pattern. It was a three-piece suit with the vest properly buttoned to display a triangle of a muted white-on-white striped silk shirt. The silk tie was silvery blue, striped diagonally with narrow, darker-blue lines. It was another giveaway—no one wore ties in Carefree, Arizona.

The long slim lines of the suit were designed to give the wearer the appearance of height, but even without the benefit of such an optical illusion, Katherine would've guessed the man to be a good two or three inches over six feet. The breadth of shoulders was almost too wide for the narrow continental lines, but she had a hunch the suit had been hand-tailored to fit the firm, lean body.

Narrow trousers tapered down long legs, which were crossed at the ankles as the man lounged against the row of brass-doored niches. He was shod in a pair of buffed gray loafers, the snaffle bit across the toe polished to a discreet pewter. While the shoes were undoubtedly expensive and designed for business attire, Katherine had the distinct impression that the exchange of the more traditional dress oxfords for these comfortable loafers was probably the greatest concession to casual dressing or living this man ever made.

Even his laconic, watchful demeanor was a carefully constructed pose, Katherine decided. There wasn't an easygoing bone in that man's body. He radiated restless energy from every male pore.

She returned her gaze back up to his face, somewhat shaken to realize he'd been observing her studied appraisal. Katherine lifted her gauze-covered shoulder in a slight, uncaring shrug. He was, after all, a stranger in these parts. Anyone who ran around Carefree dressed like that would have to get used to a few stares. She met his amber eyes boldly, refusing to acknowledge there'd been any personal interest in her examination.

The golden depths of his hooded eyes flared for a brief moment and Katherine was jolted with a shock of something akin to recognition. Something buried deep in a memory long past. A memory that seemed to insist she was acquainted with this stranger leaning against the wall of her post office with an air of detached elegance.

Impossible! She studied his face in greater detail,

deciding that if they had met, she'd have never forgotten him. It wasn't exactly a handsome face; there were far too many life experiences etched on the high planes to be considered traditionally good-looking. Yet, there was a masculine strength in the roughly hewn lines that made Katherine's toes curl in her running shoes.

The crisp dark-brown hair, in the slanting sun pouring through the glass of the front door, seemed to be shot through with a fiery, reddish tint. Katherine had the impression that, if allowed to grow a bit, his hair would probably be wavy. But the stranger seemed disinclined to spotlight this feature, and the russet hair was clipped too short for her own personal taste. Not a crew cut, by any means, but the style still screamed of conservatism, as did the rest of his appearance. Katherine wasn't a big fan of conservatism, politically or socially. A touch of silver shimmered in the sunlit brown depths, allowing her to figure his age to be somewhere in his middle to late thirties.

The one thing about the carefully groomed man that could never be considered moderate was his eyes. Tawny gold—the color of a lion's eyes. They appeared to have a life of their own as they returned her study, sparkling with undisguised interest and a lambent flame.

Katherine, in an attempt to escape the devastating gaze, followed a straight, uncompromising nose, which was honed as sharp as a Toledo blade, down to full, surprisingly sensual lips. Those lips, which were at the moment drawn into a tight line, helped soften the chiseled lines of his rugged face. She found herself idly wondering what they'd look like if they were to tilt in a welcoming smile. From there, she allowed herself a momentary fantasy of what they'd taste like and how they'd feel against her own.

Once again, Katherine was shaken by that eerie feeling that she should know. A feeling that once, as if in another lifetime, she'd experienced the pleasure of his kiss firsthand.

She shook her head, dismissing such runaway daydreams. Whoever this stranger was, she hoped he could afford a long vacation. Everything about him radiated a barely controlled male energy, as if he were a coiled spring. Or a tiger, about to pounce. She seriously doubted the man knew the meaning of the word "relax."

Katherine bade farewell as the elderly postmistress paused for breath, and made her way to the door, leafing through the stack of mail as she went. She was brought up short when the tall male form stood in her way, as effective as a human roadblock.

"K. L. Michaels?" The deep voice had a strange quality, soft and rough at the same time. Like velvet.

Katherine fought the startled, guilty flush that threatened to brighten her complexion under the smooth surface of her skin. She succeeded more in hardening her warm brown eyes to obsidian.

"I'm afraid you have the wrong person," she stated firmly, sidling deftly in order to get around him.

The stranger moved, once again blocking her forward progress. "You wouldn't happen to know a K. L. Michaels, would you?"

The silky interrogative was laced with inherent danger and Katherine fought down the unnerving feeling that the man knew more than he was prepared to let on.

"No, I wouldn't," she lied through her teeth. She

lifted her gaze to his, smiling a saccharine smile. "Is the lady a friend of yours?"

He folded his arms across the width of well-tailored chest, looking down at her with a metallic smooth gaze. "Now, if she were a friend," he suggested with maddening logic, his tone matching his eyes, "I'd have certainly known whether or not you were she. Wouldn't I?"

A flicker of movement flashed deep in his lion eyes and Katherine had the uneasy impression that laughter was lurking beneath that bronzed surface. What did he know?

"You're right, of course," she agreed briskly. "And since I'm afraid I don't know the person in question, I'd be of little help, wouldn't I?"

She did her best to hide her fear, smiling politely as she tried edging to the left this time.

"You've got a point," the man answered, moving once again, this time not to block her, but to open the door. "You know, I've always heard a great deal about western hospitality," he murmured all too close to her ear as she escaped past him. "But it's absolutely overwhelming to see it in action."

Katherine refused to acknowledge the dangerously low taunt, keeping her eyes straight ahead as she left the post office. She knew if she were to turn around, those brilliantly tawny eyes would be gleaming with a distinct, unflattering mockery.

The image of those eyes remained with her the rest of the way home, causing a rise of goose bumps on her tanned skin. Dangerous. That was the only way to describe the man. Whatever he was doing so far from his natural environs, this man meant to do her harm.

Stupid, she laughed at herself as she drove through the gates of her privately developed community and waved a greeting to the security guard. You should try writing mysteries or horror stories, instead of painting. Your imagination, girl, is working overtime!

The man was a stranger. Nothing more. Another snowbird come to escape the chills of a northern winter. The fact that he was dressed in such atypical fashion for this part of the country was the only reason she'd even noticed him.

You've been out on the range too long, K. L. Michaels, she scolded herself, opening the dead bolt with her key and letting herself into her sunny spacious home.

She'd spent the past two weeks in the northern part of the state sketching scenes of an all-Indian rodeo. During the long drive home, her mind had been busy selecting those that would become oil paintings.

It was phenomenal, this sudden surge in the popularity of western art. Three years ago, Katherine had been forced to supplement her meager painting income by making the rounds of county fairs, painting caricatures and pastel chalk drawings for two dollars apiece. A group portrait might have gone as high as a five-dollar bill.

Now, a single K. L. Michaels oil was like money in the bank. Her last painting, auctioned at the Western Heritage Sale in Houston, had brought in a mind-boggling seventy thousand dollars.

The sudden windfall hadn't made Katherine feel any differently about her work or her life. It had, however, allowed her to create a rather comfortable life-style in this custom-designed house on the sixteenth hole of the Desert Hills Golf Course. Although horribly impractical in these days of energy conservation, the house boasted of high glass walls and several skylights. At any given time, Katherine could move her easels into perfect light.

It was, perhaps, her love of light and color that had found her an audience in the growing movement of the art. Her blazing brushes captured all the vibrancy of the beautifully savage country. The panoramic scenery, bathed in dawn's early crimson, glowing light, and the pastel-hued buttes and mesas served as backdrops for her action-packed scenes. If the term "earth tones" usually referred to ambers and browns, K. L. Michaels had given a new definition to the words. She surrounded herself with vibrant, flaming colors. In her art, in her home, and in her wardrobe.

Katherine left her luggage by the door, moving down the long expanse of Mexican white tile toward her bedroom. The ocean of white was brightened every third tile by a hand-painted flower, creating the impression of a garden underfoot. She was tired from the long drive and looked forward to a long, leisurely bath. But that harsh face kept insinuating itself into her thoughts, stirring up her weary mind.

A new man in town, checking out the local female population, she thought. The male of the species always checks out the hunting ground first. It's his nature.

A pass by the high mirrored wall of her bedroom shot that argument down in flames as she stopped to peruse her appearance. The air-conditioner in her car had broken down about two hundred miles north of Carefree and she'd been forced to drive with her windows down. A thin veil of dust covered her from head to toe, the vivid exception being huge circles around her doe-brown eyes. Her raven-black hair had been pulled back into a tight braid that hung down to her waist. The tawny desert dust filtered out the deep blue luster that usually gleamed there, making it appear more like dull, anthracite coal. Her gauzy, full-sleeved blouse was a vibrant display of rainbow colors, but it too was covered with dust. Katherine wrinkled her nose, lifted a billowy sleeve to it, and sneezed violently. Her jeans were worn and wrinkled at the knees from so many hours of driving.

No, Katherine decided, shaking her head grimly, a man like that doesn't waste time on grungy desert dwellers. And his gaze hadn't been a simple impersonal male appraisal. No, there'd been that flash which had seared between them for a moment, like sulfurous sheet lightning. Her worried mind tossed the problem around, like a fallen leaf caught in a whirlpool, circling and circling, attempting to work free.

She stuffed the filthy clothing into a white wicker hamper and settled gratefully into the huge, deep tile-lined bathtub. When the tub was completely filled, the water reached her chin, one luxury acquired with her painting income that she truly adored.

K. L. Michaels. That was the problem. He was looking for her. The dark, threatening man was here in Carefree hunting for K. L. Michaels. But why?

She was listening to the messages on her telephone recorder as she unpacked when the reason for the stranger's appearance became clear.

"Katherine, I think we've got problems." It was the rapid-fire voice of the gallery owner in Manhattan where she'd just completed a successful showing and sale. "I did my best to head him off, but I don't think he fell for any of it. So keep your eyes open, sweetheart, for a man named Hunter St. James. He's been laying seige to the gallery for the past week, intent on purchasing *Spring Snow*. I've repeatedly told him it's not for sale, but the man doesn't suffer defeat gracefully. Last I heard, he was threatening to track down and deal directly with the artist. I thought he was bluffing, of course. I mean, darling, it's a nice little painting and all, but certainly not representative of your better work, if you don't mind me saying so. Anyway," the words had been coming like missiles and Katherine heard the deep intake of breath as Donald Waring geared up for a second wind.

"Anyway, Katherine, after that threat, there settled an unnatural calm around our little gallery. Sort of like the lull before the storm. I'm beginning to think he may have actually taken off for Arizona. On the slight chance he manages to find his way to Carefree, I'd keep an eye out for him. He's not a very nice man, Katherine. If you know what I mean."

"Oh, yes, Donald," Katherine murmured, turning off the machine with a flick. "I know exactly what you mean. You're right. I don't think he's a very nice man."

His mother must have been blessed with second sight, naming the man Hunter, she mused silently. A more natural predator, Katherine Michaels had never laid eyes on.

She was just thanking her lucky stars that her newly acquired wealth had allowed for this securely protected house, flanked by the security guard at those tall gates, when the intercom buzzed, slicing into her thoughts. Moving over to the wall speaker, Katherine flipped the switch.

"Yes, Jack." She acknowledged the call with the inevitability of one who's accepted the contest about to take place. "Who's there?"

"A stranger, Miss Michaels. Looks like an easterner.

All duded up in a suit and such. Anyway, the fella's asking for K. L. Michaels. I told him there's nobody here by that name, but he insisted K. L. Michaels would be expecting him. Name is Hunter St. James."

There was an obvious question in the last statement and Katherine blessed him silently for his discretion. "I'm not expecting any such person, Jack. But if he gives you any problems, please let me know."

"Yes'm. Don't you worry. I'll get rid of him."

Katherine flipped the switch off and paced the room, a plum-hued nail between her wide, white teeth as she waited him out. Hunter St. James wouldn't surrender the chase easily. She'd have to be prepared for his next assault.

She knew he'd receive no information from anyone in town. The community had its share of famous people, but while everyone was friendly and outgoing, all had the unique ability to mind their own business.

Many of the residents were writers or artists, working under pseudonyms, and privacy was respected as essential. It would never do, for example, to have the patients of a well-known internist discover the good doctor wrote bodice-rippers, those historical novels consisting of rakish pirates and ravished maidens. So Victoria Witherspoon's secret remained safely hidden away within Dr. Dennis Lawton's walled estate. And that tenured economics professor who'd turned to academia after a brilliant career in high-finance—he certainly wouldn't want it to become common knowledge that he was a free-lance contributor to an illustrated teenage humor magazine. No, the community, while close, knew how to keep its secrets. A virtue that Katherine had her own reasons to appreciate.

Finally, after a long, quiet pause, she decided that the gallery owner had, as usual, been overreacting.

Whoever Hunter St. James was, the man seemed unwilling to precipitate a direct confrontation. When met with his first real obstacle, he'd retreated. But why would he have come all the way to Arizona only to give up so easily?

Katherine shrugged and returned her attention to the rest of the recorded messages. Obviously the man had planned on making the trip, either for business or vacation, and decided to try to meet her at the same time. So much for a pair of overactive imaginations running amuck! The next time she was in New York, she and Donald would have to share a good laugh over their mistaken fears.

Katherine was making three lists. The first one was of calls that had to be answered immediately. The second, calls that could be put off a day or two. And the third, calls that required no answer. When she was well into the third list, the familiar, unmistakable sound of shattering glass captured her attention. Katherine sighed, rising from her chair to move into the adjoining room.

A distinct disadvantage in residing near the sixteenth hole of the rolling, hilltop golf course was the water hazard. All too often, in an attempt to overcompensate for the small, ball-filled lake, golfers would send the hard white ball flying through her french doors. Or the glass wall on either side. Luckily, she noted, as she eyed the small shards of safety glass on the tile floor, this errant duffer had gotten the door.

Katherine extracted the ball from its glittering surroundings and opened the door, to wait for the golfer, whom she knew from experience would be frantic and apologetic. She tossed it up, catching it in her open palm repeatedly, eyeing the brilliant wintergreen grass expectantly. She'd grown used to this. It was the price one paid for having access to acres of verdant green right outside your door.

Katherine almost dropped the ball on its downward path, her free hand flying to her throat as she eyed the golfer striding toward her, club swinging loosely in his hand. The Italian gray suit was certainly not appropriate golf-course attire. And the triumphant, amber-gold stare wasn't the gaze of a man simply out for a relaxing day on the links.

Chapter Two

Katherine could hear her teeth grinding together as she prepared for the impending battle. Guerrilla warfare, she considered, watching Hunter St. James draw nearer, with a self-assured stride. Donald had been right after all. This was not a very nice man.

"Your ball, I believe." Katherine managed a bland tone as she held it out to him.

"What a coincidence," he offered by way of greeting. "We meet again." He looked past her shoulder into the spacious, sun-filled room. "Do you live here?"

Hunter took the ball from her outstretched hand and slipped it into a jacket pocket. His tailor would kill him for that, she thought, eyeing the material as it bulged out of shape.

"Somehow I don't believe it's such a coincidence," she retorted, her voice frosted with a sharp, icy edge. "May I ask why you're following me around, Mr.—" Katherine's jaw snapped shut just in time as she remembered she wasn't supposed to know his name.

"St. James," he offered. "Hunter St. James. And you're—?" A dark red-brown brow arched, waiting for her to admit what Katherine realized he'd already determined.

"Why are you here, Mr. St. James? Or would you like to save yourself the trouble of repeating your little tale and just wait until the police arrive?"

A good defense was always a strong offense. And with the apparent strength of her opponent, Katherine needed to use every trick she knew.

"Do you call out the cops everytime someone breaks one of your windows with a golf ball?" He overrode her threat with a note of disbelief.

"Of course not! What we're discussing here is the fact that you've been following me, and I consider that harassment. And invasion of privacy, not to mention trespassing." Her voice rose to an unnaturally strident pitch and Katherine glanced around, realizing she'd caught the interested attention of a golfing foursome.

"Wrong." Hunter contradicted her smoothly, his white teeth showing in a glimmer of a smile that reminded her of a shark. There was certainly no warmth in the expression. "I've been following K. L. Michaels. So, unless you happen to be the aforesaid western artist, I couldn't have possibly been following you. Now, why don't we continue this little conversation indoors before you're forced to sell tickets?"

Katherine opened her mouth in sheer disbelief as he moved past her with all the physical arrogance of a panther. Once in the living room, he picked up the stack of mail. "Katherine Lorene Michaels. Interesting. Quite a coincidence, wouldn't you say?"

She snatched the letters from his hand. "What are you doing here, Mr. St. James?"

"That depends. My business is with K. L. Michaels. I'm not willing to discuss it with an impostor."

"Impostor!" Two furious red flags waved in her cheeks. "I'll have you know there's a very good reason for my keeping my identity a secret!" Katherine's dark eyes flashed at the man who'd been causing her nothing but grief all day.

"I'm sure there is," he murmured, "but I'm not really interested. What I am interested in, miss—it is miss, isn't it?" he asked suddenly, casting an appraising glance at her hands, which were adorned with sparkling rings, none of which remotely resembled a wedding band.

"Ms.," Katherine said, curtly. What business was it of his, anyway?

"What I'm here for," Hunter continued, "is to arrange the purchase of *Spring Snow*."

"That painting isn't for sale, Mr. St. James." She made her tone even chillier. "I believe that was made perfectly clear at the Waring Gallery." Katherine turned her back on him, moving to the front door, and opened it widely. "I'm sorry if you've made the trip out here for nothing, but I'm not interested in selling *Spring Snow*. At any price." She folded her arms, waiting silently for him to take the hint and leave.

"Oh, everyone has a price, Ms. Michaels. Now, why don't you just close that door so we can sit down and discuss yours?"

Katherine's mouth flew open in astonishment. She was about to blister him with a few well-chosen suggestions about what he could do instead when someone rushed in through the door.

"Katherine! Where in the world have you been? You haven't answered a single call!"

The tall, willowy woman with a flaming orange mane of hair swept into the room, a crocheted caftan skimming over her bikini-clad body, allowing enticing hints of bronzed skin.

"I was just getting to them," Katherine said with a

curt, impolite nod in Hunter St. James' direction, "when I was interrupted."

Emerald-green eyes outlined with a sweeping slash of black kohl followed Katherine's glare. "Well, I don't blame you. I'd allow myself to get interrupted too." The woman moved across the room with the swinging, toes-out stride peculiar to dancers, her hand outstretched and a broad smile on her poppy-red lips.

"Hello," the throaty voice offered, the bright-green eyes making an overt appraisal of the tall, lean male form. "I knew Katherine was big on feeding the migrating fowl which land on that lake"—the auburn head nodded toward the sparkling blue water beyond the glass wall—"but I hadn't realized she'd begun taking in snowbirds. I'm Monica Bradshaw. And welcome. You're going to be a terrific addition to our little village."

Monica turned toward Katherine with obvious approval. "He's going to do wonders for this season," she predicted, her eyes practically screaming her congratulatory message.

"Hunter St. James," he replied in introduction, taking the outstretched hand in both of his as those tawny gold eyes met the emerald appraisal. His mouth deepened attractively in a magic smile, suddenly transforming the harshly planed face. Katherine could only stare dumbly at the potent charm he was bestowing upon her best friend. Once again, she experienced that strange shock of recognition, but she still couldn't place it.

"I'm sorry I kept Kate from your emergency," the deep voice apologized. Katherine kept staring, wondering just how often those full sensual lips offered up anything even resembling repentance. But, she considered with good nature, Monica had always been able to wrap men around her little finger. "I'm afraid we easterners aren't renowned for our patience," the smooth baritone tones continued to roll smoothly off the treacherous tongue. "I had a problem of my own which kept me from considering that there might be someone else with prior claim to Kate's time."

"Kate?" A penciled auburn brow rose at the name. "How well did you say you two knew each other?" Bright-green eyes moved from Hunter's bland expression to Katherine's confused one.

"I just met him, Monica," Katherine snapped. "And as you can see, Mr. St. James doesn't even know me well enough to realize I only go by Katherine. Or Ms. Michaels." She shot him a threatening glance, but was only answered by a brief, mocking nod and a low, insinuating murmur.

"Or K. L. Michaels."

"Well, whatever." Monica's attention moved back to herself, obviously unable to decipher the latent hostility around them. "I've got a problem only you can solve," she proclaimed, settling down onto the magenta sofa with the inherent grace of a grand duchess. She stretched her slender arms along the top and crossed long legs in a fluid, graceful movement. Katherine couldn't help noticing that every gesture was an invitation to the silent, watchful stranger, but she also knew that Monica wasn't consciously attempting to seduce Hunter St. James.

The two women had been friends since childhood and Katherine knew that Monica's seductiveness was second nature. As natural as breathing. She'd always seemed honestly shocked, even apologetic, to discover she'd ended up with yet another of Katherine's boyfriends. Katherine's dark eyes slid surreptitiously to Hunter, noting that he had that familiar glazed expression on his face. There goes another one, she sighed inwardly. Then she gave herself a swift mental kick.

Another one? They weren't high-school seniors, for heaven's sake. And nothing could remotely qualify this horrid man as a boyfriend! What in heaven's name was he doing to her thoughts? The thing to do was get him out of here. Now!

"Monica, I don't think this is the time—"

"Honey, I don't have any more time. I've been trying to reach you for ten days. I take it you were out roaming the range with the deer and the antelope again." The disapproving tone indicated very well what the elegant woman thought of Katherine's propensity to travel to the outreaches of civilization.

"I was up at Window Rock." She nodded.

"Well, I'm in a helluva bind and you're absolutely the *only* person who can save my life. You know, of course, that the Cactus Flower Ballet has been drowning in red ink."

Katherine nodded, wondering what this had to do with her. She made a great deal of money, granted, but not enough to bail the floundering ballet company out of its financial hole.

"Well, there's a marvelously eccentric Arab in town. I met him at a little bash I threw for potential investors two weeks ago. I figured, with all the rich snowbirds landing, I might as well attempt to pluck a few— Oh, dear!" Her hand flew to her mouth in obvious distress as she swiveled her flaming head in Hunter's direction. "My God, I'm sorry," Monica gasped. She was usually in control whenever there was a man around and Katherine knew it was only proof of her distress that she'd made such an amusing *faux pas*. "I didn't mean . . ."

Hunter only offered a wry grin of acceptance. "Don't mind me. I'm beginning to realize that I'm a mixed blessing around these parts. Mrs. Drake was quite succinct. And loud."

"That old biddy only arrived in 1975," Monica scoffed. "Yet to hear her gripe about newcomers, you'd think she came in a covered wagon instead of a Ford Fairmont. Don't pay a bit of attention to her, Hunter. You're going to be a four-star attraction, once we get you out and circulating."

Hunter caught Katherine's eye, tawny devils dancing in his gaze. She glared back.

"Well, anyway," Monica returned her rather flightly line of thought to the problem at hand. "This darling man has offered us five-hundred thousand dollars." She drawled the sum out, obviously relishing the sound of the extravagant figure. "We'll be able to perform *Sleeping Beauty* on schedule."

"Half a million dollars? Is the man crazy?"

"No, just filthy rich. Poor dear has more money than he knows what to do with. Those delightful little oil wells keep bubbling up that delicious crude somewhere over in the Middle East, and there appears to be no end. Ahmed is forced to find new ways to spend all the lovely money."

"Poor dear," Katherine said dryly. "It must be exhausting. So, what's the problem? It sounds as if you're all set."

"Well, there's just one teensy little thing." Monica flashed Katherine a brilliant, theatrical smile and Katherine knew she wasn't going to get out of this one easily.

"What's this one *little* thing?"

"He so admired the painting of those Hopi dancers I have on my wall, that he's bought three of your paintings from End of the Trail." She named a local gallery.

"Great. I'm pleased to be able to help the man find new outlets for his funds."

"Well, he admired them so. He just loves our American west, you know—"

"Monica. Why don't you just tell me what you need?"

"He wants to meet you at the party I'm having in his honor tomorrow night." The words tumbled out from the poppy-red lips as if they could somehow slip past Katherine's conscious mind undetected.

"Impossible."

"Katherine—" Monica's voice immediately fell into a wheedling tone Katherine recognized. She'd heard it for the first time when both women were six years old and Monica had needed her to play the role of the wolf in an amateur production of *Little Red Riding Hood*. Monica, of course, had been Little Red Riding Hood.

Katherine shook her head firmly. "You know how I feel about publicity. I will not, even for you, allow it to become common knowledge that K. L. Michaels is a woman. If I attend your little bash and let you introduce me to your Ahmed, he'll boast at other jet-set affairs that he's met the elusive K. L. Michaels. And people who travel in his circles represent some of my biggest sales: easterners who enjoy having their taste of the American West on their walls, while they continue to proclaim Atlantic coastal supremacy."

She cast a scathing glance at Hunter, who only reacted to her pointed accusation with a bland expression.

"Katherine, *please*. You have to help me out. You are my very best friend in the entire wide world!"

"Monica, what you're asking me to do could affect my entire career."

"What I'm asking you to do, Katherine," the pouty, theatrical tone was gone, replaced by a serious honesty, "will definitely affect my career. If I can't introduce our desert bedouin to K. L. Michaels, he's leaving. With his money. Adiós Cactus Flower Ballet Company. I'm too old to go back to New York and start pounding the pavement for work, kiddo."

Katherine could tell the regret and fear was genuine and she sighed heavily. "Let me think about it. I'll call you this evening."

The tall, reedlike woman rose from the chair gracefully, coming over to kiss Katherine on the cheek. "I know you'll come through, honey. We always have for each other, right?" Her emerald eyes glistened wetly, and Katherine knew her friend wasn't acting this time.

"Right." She slumped against the door, watching as Monica waved a quick good-bye to Hunter.

"She's got a real problem," he offered into the swirling silence.

"You're right about that. So do I."

"I've got a question." The deep rich voice fell between them, and he waited for her to pick up his bait.

Katherine was bone-tired and her head was aching with everything that had transpired today. She was in no mood to play games.

"Funny," she snapped. "I thought you were the man with all the answers."

She plopped down on the couch, not inviting Hunter to do the same. A mistake, she realized immediately as she was forced to look a long way up at him. She'd inadvertently placed herself in a position of inferiority.

"Sit down." She waved her hand at a modern Danish chrome and white-leather chair. She didn't have any expectations for this discussion, but it could only go easier if he was on level ground with her.

Hunter's gaze narrowed suspiciously. "Do you sit on it or ride it?"

"For heaven's sake, don't you have modern Danish furniture in New York?"

"I don't." The firm tone announced that not only did he not possess a single piece, he didn't approve of the clean, body-contoured lines in the first place.

"Well, you can sit on the floor for all I care. But I don't intend to get a crick in my neck looking up at you like this."

Hunter lowered the tall frame distrustfully into position on the white leather, looking decidedly uncomfortable at his knees jutted up beside his body.

"You look ridiculous." A slight breath of laughter escaped her as he perched on the bent metal frame, appearing for all the world as if he were in immediate danger of being bitten by the chair.

"This furniture is ridiculous," he muttered, opting for the expanse of white Mexican tile. He leaned back on his elbows, spreading long, gray-clad legs out in front of him. "Hard," he stated, "but better. Now why won't you sell me *Spring Snow*?"

"That's personal. Why do you want it so badly?"

"That's personal."

Silence swirled around them for a time, a lingering, living thing.

"Well," Katherine finally offered, growing uncomfortable at the apparent standoff, "I suppose we've nothing further to talk about."

"No. I suppose not."

"Then, I'll say good-bye. I really have to finish listening to my messages."

"Fine. Go ahead." The long frame didn't shift position on the tile floor.

"Mr. St. James, you have to go now."

"I'm not going until you agree to sell me *Spring Snow*, Kate. It's that simple."

She leaped from the couch, coming to stand above him, her hands curled into tight fists on her hips. She'd slipped into a long terry-cloth shift after her bath, the stripes of royal blue and emerald as bold and bright as an Arab's tent. The material pulled tightly across the softly rounded swell of her stomach as she clenched it.

"Nice," he commented softly, his golden eyes gleaming with male approval and an unnerving desire. "Who'd ever suspect that K. L. Michaels, painter of Indians, cowboys, and the machismo life of the old wild West could be such a decidedly feminine woman?"

The liquid notes reached up to flow over her and Katherine fought against the sensations those molten gold eyes were making her feel. Why did she sense, again, that she knew this man?

"No one," she managed to say, "and I want to keep it that way. I believe my work wouldn't sell if people discovered I wasn't a man."

"I don't agree with you. But I can see your sincere, if rather convoluted, reasoning."

"Convoluted!"

"Convoluted." The dark head nodded, as if satisfied with his description. "But what are you going to do about your friend? I take it the two of you are very close."

More than close, Katherine admitted silently, realizing it was her turn to save the other's life. Monica had taken Katherine in after her divorce, invited her to Arizona, and helped banish the lingering pain and bitterness with a steady stream of laughter, parties, and goodwill. Living in such an atmosphere of constant gaiety, Katherine had eventually found that feeling sorry for herself was just too much of an effort.

"Let's drown the bastard," had been Monica's first words as Katherine had stepped off the plane, a newly divorced and emotionally battered young woman. Monica had led her into the airport cocktail lounge and they'd ended up spending sixty dollars on the cab ride from Phoenix Sky Harbor Airport to the town of Carefree. Even in their dazed state, both women had wisely decreed neither of them was in any shape to drive Monica's gray Mercedes. Katherine definitely owed her one. But why, oh why, did it have to be this one?

Then her attention turned back to the man lounging almost prone on her floor. Once again her dark-brown eyes moved from the top of the reddish-glinted dark hair, right down to the highly buffed loafers. Not bad, she thought. He must be a western-art buff, considering how badly he wanted *Spring Snow*. He was obviously intelligent, articulate, and no one around here knew him. Including Monica's Arab sheikh. Yes, it just might work.

"I'll tell you what," she said slowly, her mind working out the details as she spoke. Yes, it should work. Just for a few hours, of course, but that was all she needed. "I'll agree to sell you *Spring Snow*, Mr. St. James, on one condition."

"And that is?" Hunter was eyeing her warily, as a warden might watch a cellblock full of dangerous felons. She'd not been the slightest bit polite so far. Her sudden agreeable attitude seemed to be alerting him to impending danger.

"You agree to be me. K. L. Michaels. A decidedly male K. L. Michaels." She dropped her bombshell and sat back against the hard back of the magenta sofa, awaiting his response.

"A masquerade party." He sat up now, wrapping his arms about bent knees. Katherine could practically see the wheels turning as he considered it. "I think it's entirely unnecessary," he decreed, "since I'm sure your work sells on the strength of your talent, but it just might work. How about your friends? Won't they say anything?"

"Mr. St. James," Katherine answered slowly, "I'm assuming you attempted the same routine with Mrs. Drake, that you tried with Jack at the gate."

"Guilty," he acknowledged instantly. "As well as a few of the local population, including the editor of the town paper. Is everyone's privacy so closely guarded around here?"

"Everyone's. It comes with the territory."

"Nice little system." He nodded. "I suppose there's no one in town who'd admit to a living soul that you're K. L. Michaels?"

"Not a one. Why?" she asked, suddenly suspicious.

The gray-clad shoulder lifted in a lazy, dismissing shrug, which didn't completely expunge her distrust of this man.

"Just wondering. Now, don't you think you should call Monica and let her know she's off the hook?"

Monica loved the idea, finding the entire charade a delight. She agreed instantly to introduce Hunter as K. L. Michaels.

"It's probably just as well." She laughed before hanging up. "When you meet the little gold mine, you'll discover he's the quintessential male chauvinist. He'd probably roll over and drop dead to find out that he's just laid out a small fortune for cowboy paintings by a woman."

Katherine put the receiver back into its cradle and turned toward Hunter, who'd been roaming the room, observing the bright paintings on the walls. He seemed intent on one she'd done of a bronc rider, the cowboy's saddle in his hand as he viewed the horse he'd just drawn for the last ride of the day. Her dark eyes moved from canvas to the lean, rangy man studying it, realizing just how much the two men seemed to have in common.

Oh, not the clothes, certainly. The cowhand's faded jeans and shirt had nothing in common with the impeccable lines of Hunter's tailored silk suit. And she doubted the man in her living room had ever held a saddle such as the man in the painting carried. Perhaps, she allowed acidly, a polo pony was more Hunter St. James' style.

But the firm arrogant set of the jaw and the unflinching glint of determination in the eye was the same. That was something both men shared in spades. Along with a lean, steely masculine strength. Hunter St. James might not meet his daily challenges in the dusty arena of a rodeo ring, but Katherine had no doubt that he did meet them. And he'd ride them out to the bell, everytime.

"Those clothes are all wrong," she mused aloud as her finger traced the full line of her lip thoughtfully.

Hunter turned slowly, his hands thrust deep into his front pockets. "I'm sorry you disapprove. I should have realized you were an expert on male apparel. Being so chic in your own dress, of course."

His smooth amber eyes followed the lines of swirling emerald and indigo terry cloth from her breasts down to the wine-polished toes of her bare feet.

"I wasn't expecting company," she reminded him sharply. She felt like some type of ruffian in such a vivid contrast to his own immaculate appearance. "But you're overdressed."

"I wasn't expecting to have to sit on the floor."

"I have chairs, Mr. St. James."

"You have torture racks," he corrected without missing a beat. "Look, if I'm going to be taking over your identity, I'll need to know everything about you, Kate. That entitles you, in turn, to call me Hunter."

The deeply set topaz eyes seemed to be inviting her to more than the familiarity of his name, and Katherine had to concentrate in order to jerk her attention back to the problem at hand.

"You just don't look like a western artist," she complained, walking around him slowly, her judicious gaze trying to remain impersonally studious.

"Neither do you," he reminded her. "According to your rather strict standards, that is."

"I don't suppose you have anything western?" she asked hopefully, knowing it was a futile wish.

The corner of his mouth quirked slightly as his eyes echoed the humor. "Do I look as though I'd own any western clothing?"

Katherine shook her ebony head, her long braid swinging like a length of glossy rope. She'd washed it after bathing and rebraided it while it was still wet.

Now, dry and free of its earlier dust, it gleamed in the late-afternoon sun like sparkling jet.

"No," she sighed, "you don't. And here I thought everyone in New York was into the Urban Cowboy look. I suppose it would've been too easy for you to have been more fad-oriented." Her voice was a cross between an accusation and a condemnation.

"Not only too easy," he admitted smoothly, "but too ridiculous. Every attorney, cardiologist, and advertising exec is running around Manhattan dressed up like Roy Roger clones. It looks like some kind of invasion of the rhinestone cowboy people. No, thanks, honey, I'm not into impersonating other people. Unless, of course, they're delightful western artists with a proclivity for deception."

Chapter Three

Gold suddenly flared in Hunter's eyes and Katherine found herself rooted to the spot as her eyes became locked in the swirling amber depths. Hunter strode determinedly toward her. His hand reached out and she flinched in response. It wasn't fear of him harming her that caused the involuntary reaction.

Katherine realized as she'd pulled away that the instinct was far more primitive. She was afraid of the feeling this man's touch might evoke within her. The gold in the hypnotizing eyes flared higher, melting her helplessly in the molten gaze.

"Shhh," he crooned softly as his hands touched her shoulders in a heartbreakingly gentle caress. "Don't be so afraid of me." The honey-warm tone was familiar to her. She'd heard it often used to calm nervous fillies. "Trust me, Kate."

Trust him? Trust a man who was endowed with such barely restrained primal forces as this man possessed? Trust a man who'd instilled terror in the milk-toast heart of a Manhattan gallery owner? Trust a man who'd literally smashed his way into her home? Oh, God. Trust a man who was lifting the thick swathe of glossy black hair and holding it lightly in the cradle of his palm, as if testing its weight?

Katherine drew in a sharp breath as he took the long braid and feathered her throbbing pulse at the base of her throat with its soft, silky tip. She'd tied the end with a royal-blue satin ribbon, leaving a three-inch fan of freed hair that was now being used to tease her in a strangely seductive way. His eyes remained on hers, savoring the helpless response his caresses were receiving as he brushed the sensuous weapon along her collarbone and down the slight swell of her breasts.

"Hunter, don't do that . . . You have no right."

"Hush, Kate," he murmured, his eyes leading hers into a satiny, sensual dance. "I've every right."

Katherine's mind was rapidly becoming intoxicated by the glowing amber eyes, the tantalizing caresses, and Hunter's decidedly male scent, which rose about her head like a thick cloud of sweet incense. She tried to concentrate on his crooning words, tried to decipher their cryptic meaning, but to no avail.

His long fingers slid the ribbon from the braid, moving through the tight tresses to loosen her hair, and fanning it out so that it flowed over her shoulders and down her back in an ebony waterfall. The tight braiding had created soft waves and his hands moved through the silky length, settling it over her shoulders as his palms followed it down to caress her breasts.

"Oh!" Katherine's senses were jolted with the intensity of an electric shock as those hands closed over her full breasts, his fingers playing with the soft flesh.

"You're mine, Kate. We've both known it from the moment you walked into that post office. I don't intend to have us repeat past mistakes, darling."

"Past mistakes?" she asked dazedly, feeling the

erotic response of her nipples to his increasingly intimate caress.

He tilted the dark head back to look at her. "You really don't know?"

Words were too difficult. Katherine only shook her head.

For a moment it appeared that Hunter would explain his mysterious statement. But as his gaze moved over her uplifted face, the golden flames sparked to an incredible height in his tawny eyes and his lips lowered to hers. His kiss claimed her with the same intensity as the fire that flared in his eyes. Her attempt at refusal was buried in her throat as the bruising force of his mouth silenced her. Katherine twisted her head, attempting to break free of the hard, intimate contact, but strong hands tangled in her long, unbound hair, holding her still.

There was no evading the mouth that ground so passionately against hers, so possessively. But once she'd survived the shocking impact, Katherine began to sense that Hunter wasn't seeking to harm her. That feeling was enhanced by the low, tortured sounds deep in his throat.

Hunter St. James was kissing her with an urgent, undeniable need, as if he were overcome with a pain only Katherine could possibly transform to pleasure. As if he'd been carrying this hunger with him for a long time, seeking her out to ease his starving senses.

There was harsh, agonized longing in every hard, taut line of this man. Although it made no sense to her, the very idea that she was capable of driving a man to such despair that he'd display this raw emotion created an explosive response. With the violence of a bursting dam, Katherine's own hunger flared, and she flung her arms about his neck, pressing her soft feminine shape into his aroused male hardness. Her mouth opened, no longer in protest, but in hot invitation. Blood surged through her veins as Hunter sought out and engaged her tongue in a savage, twisting duel.

"Hunter ... my God," Katherine cried out in uninhibited wonder as he dragged his mouth from hers, his lips and teeth nibbling at every bit of skin as they burned a flaming brand from one bared shoulder to the other. Her fingers thrust through his crisp, dark hair, her body moving in undulating, desperate circles as it strived for even more contact.

Her heart was beating like a snare drum as his lips moved lower and the darting, flicking tongue reached down to taste the warm shadow between her breasts. Her fevered mind threatened to lose its last grip on sanity as she was buffeted in the storm this man had created about them. Katherine's hands moved under the charcoal-gray jacket and around to his back, where she clutched him, her fingernails making harsh, desperate paths along his spine.

She didn't object as he lowered her to the firm surface of the sofa, pressing her soft fluid curves into the molded cushions. She didn't object as he pulled the top of her terry caftan down, treating her full breasts to his burning, unsatiated gaze as he sat poised over her. But as his knee moved to part her thighs, and his fingers became busy on the bright buttons, Katherine grasped at her last thread of sanity.

"Hunter! This is too soon!"

His hands froze on the buttons, pressing lightly into the soft skin of her abdomen. The last glittering rays of the day's sun glanced off his eyes, turning the swirling browns and golds to a shimmering display.

He was watching her with the intensity that a circling hawk might use to study its prey.

"May I take that to mean that you'll be willing later?"

"How can I answer that? I don't even know you."

Hunter pulled the brilliant terry back over her breasts, reluctant acquiescence shadowing the gleaming desire. "You know me," he returned with soft conviction.

Katherine's eyes were dark wells as she sought to understand. "How can you say that? We just met."

He ran his hand down her body, from her full, love-rounded breasts to her knee and back up again, his fingers lingering along the heated trail as if he'd like to revoke his compliance with her wishes.

"You know me," he repeated, his gaze lingering for an uncomfortably long time on her full, slightly bruised lips. "Just as I know everything I need to know about you." There was such a deep strain of male arrogance in his tone that Katherine wiggled abruptly out from under him and sat up.

"I'm not a big one for playing games, Hunter. I'd like an explanation. You've been hinting at some imagined intimacy and I'm fed up with veiled insinuations: so out with it, now!"

Her growing anger wasn't helped by the gleam she saw dancing in the depths of his eyes or that lazy, self-confident grin.

"Now, now, Kate. Don't get all riled up. We've all night to talk about the past. And the future."

"All night!" She was on her knees on the magenta cushion, glaring down at him. "We've nothing of the kind. I've had a very long day and I'd like to get to sleep early." Katherine gave herself bonus points for avoiding the word "bed." That would've been too easy for him.

Hunter's hand stroked her thigh. "That's fine with me, honey. You go ahead. I'll just lie beside you and watch."

Her eyes widened, as large and brown as a startled doe. "Hunter, I sleep alone. I want you to go home now. Where are you staying, anyway?"

"The inn," he answered as his hand moved in enticing circles on the soft swell of her stomach. "But it's too quiet around there."

"That's what you're paying all that money for," she pointed out, picking up the seductive hand and placing it back into his own lap. "They go to great lengths to achieve that aura of genteel tranquillity."

"Well, it's too damn tranquil. I'm not used to being able to hear my own breathing," he mumbled. "It's like living in a graveyard."

Katherine shook her head, laughing at the honest, distressed look on his strong features. "Do you realize you've just committed a cardinal sin? Insulting the inn like that? It's a landmark hotel."

"It's a mausoleum," he countered. "I get nervous when I'm surrounded by so much peace and quiet."

"It's simply withdrawal symptoms," she diagnosed, patting him lightly on the cheek, her palm encountering the scratchy feel of his late-afternoon beard. "Just take your time and decompress slowly. That way you won't get the bends."

"You're really going to kick me out?" His look was definitely accusing, but still held just a hint of appeal.

"Don't put it so harshly, Hunter. There are millions of people who would hardly consider sending you back to the inn as sentencing you to prison."

He sighed and lifted his trim body from the sofa.

"You're going to spend the night kicking youself for not begging me to stay." His words were said with supreme confidence, and he suddenly walked across the white tile that led to the hallway.

Katherine could feel the anger rising higher as her hands curled into fists. For two cents, she'd tell this arrogant man to get the hell out of her life. In fact, she'd tell him to get the hell out of town, but she needed him. For now. However, after the party tomorrow night, she'd have no further use for his services and she'd get on with her pleasant, well-ordered life.

She took off after him and found him in the bathroom, checking his appearance in the mirror. Katherine leaned against the door jamb, arms crossed over her terry-clad chest.

"We need to get you some new clothes. Come by tomorrow morning and we'll go shopping," she instructed.

"You buying?" His tawny eyes narrowed.

"I've only agreed to sell you a painting, Hunter. I didn't agree to keep you," she retorted lightly.

He picked up her comb and ran it through the short, crisp dark hair. There was an intimacy in the casual way he shared possession of the comb that unnerved her. He caught her troubled gaze in the mirror, amber eyes meeting brown.

"It's not the money," he argued softly, still looking at her in the glass. "It's the principle of the thing. Why should I have to buy clothing I'll never wear again for a party I wasn't even invited to? I'm doing this as a favor to you, Kate," he reminded her silkily. Hunter gave the comb one more quick pass, then nodded in satisfaction and put it down on the marble-topped counter.

"You're doing it so I'll sell you *Spring Snow*."

"Perhaps," he agreed laconically, turning to face her, "but, I'm not in the market for a cowboy suit, Kate. Maybe you'd better find someone who already has a pair of chaps hanging up in his closet."

"All right," Katherine shot back, her dark eyes turning to black glass. "I'll buy the damn clothes."

"Thank you, darling. That's very generous." Hunter grinned unrepentantly at the way he'd backed her into the neat, tight corner.

"Be here early," she rasped out, marching him to the front door.

"Six o'clock early enough?"

Her raven brows rose high on her forehead before crashing down. "Six o'clock? In the *morning*?" Katherine knew such an hour existed, it was just that she'd always done her best to avoid meeting it.

"Too late?"

"Too early. Make it ten."

"Ten o'clock can hardly be described as early." Hunter leaned against the door jamb, obviously prepared to argue yet another point. Dear Lord, did the man have to challenge everything?

"You'd never get away with that in New York, Kate. The trash collectors start banging cans before it's light. I think they do it for spite. If they're up and working, the rest of the city better be, too."

"It sounds delightful," Katherine commented dryly, moving to shut the door on him. "Absolute nirvana. I can see why you miss it so much, Hunter."

He moved, allowing the hand-carved Spanish mahogany door to close on him. As she finally shut him from her house, Katherine leaned back against the door, exhaling with deep relief. What had she gotten herself into?

She soon found that locking the dark-haired, amber-eyed man out entirely was an impossibility. He followed her into the kitchen, where she fixed herself a plate of peanut-butter crackers and a glass of milk. Then he accompanied her to bed, where she turned on the television and sat, watching an old movie while eating her light suppper.

He continued to tease her seductively as she tried to concentrate on the light, 1930s black-and-white comedy. Finally, brushing the sprinkling of crumbs from the bed, Katherine aimed her remote control at the screen and extinguished the flickering image. If only, she thought as she burrowed down into her pillows, it were that easy to expunge Hunter St. James from her mind's eye. He hovered there, teasing her, threatening her, and ultimately seducing her, throughout the fitful, unsatisfying sleep.

Hunter rang the doorbell promptly at ten o'clock, looking as if he'd been pacing circles outside for hours. The energy emanating from the man was almost electric, managing to tire her before the day had even begun. Katherine had called down to Jack last night, leaving Hunter's name at the gate. Obviously, since he was standing in her doorway, he'd encountered no trouble. At least it would save her additional panes of glass.

"Would you like some coffee?"

"I think I've already had about two pots," he confessed, a wry grin on his face. "I'm not used to the leisurely life, I'm afraid. Relaxing only seems to make me nervous."

"New Yorkers!" She shook her dark head.

"You don't approve of us?"

"I don't disapprove of you," Katherine said, moving

toward the kitchen, knowing Hunter would follow. "It's just not the way I prefer to live my life."

"How do you know?" he asked with apparent interest.

"I tried it," Katherine answered simply, pouring herself a mug of the coffee. She turned toward him, leaning against the counter as she sipped it.

"Really?" Amber eyes narrowed as Hunger aimed his perceptive gaze across the intervening space. "I never would've guessed that."

She eyed him over the rim of the mug, replying with a half-shrug. "I've put those days behind me. They were a long time ago, and I was a different woman."

Hunter pulled out a chair, straddling it, his arms resting on the back as he favored her with a particularly sagacious look. "Was it that bad?"

Katherine cradled the rainbow mug in her hands and considered the question thoughtfully. It had been almost five years since she'd stepped off the plane that had carried her from her shattered life in New York City. The years and her work had done their healing well, she realized. It no longer hurt to talk about it.

"It seemed so at the time," she admitted. "Now, looking back, I'd say it was probably no worse than anyone else's bad times."

"Were you an artist then?"

Katherine laughed at the question. "What's the matter, Hunter? Can't you see me painting anything but cowboys?"

The smooth grave tones were unsettling. "I can see you painting anything you wanted, and making a success of it. You managed to capture Spring Snow—body, mind and soul. You brought her to life for me,

Kate. After seeing that, I don't have a single doubt as to your abilities."

Katherine digested the remark silently, surprised by the fervor of his answer to her lighthearted inquiry. She sipped the strong black brew, welcoming the caffeine it was sending through her bloodstream in awakening jolts. As if he weren't enough of an impact to start all her senses stirring, she thought. Even seated, he seemed to be filling the sunny room with his strength.

The long tightly corded legs stretched out in front of him were encased in a deep, bark-brown slacks, the loafers today a dark saddle brown. His silk shirt was the color of freshly churned country cream and was covered with a soft suede jacket reminiscent of buttered rum. A dark-brown knit tie completed the look, which, while more casual than the gray suit of yesterday, was still far more formal than anything usually seen in Carefree. Her fingers were itching to pull that tie from around his neck and to unbutton the collar of the shirt so she could get a glimpse of his dark skin. Just a glimpse. And maybe a slight touch, she added. The memory of his heady masculine scent returned as her thoughts continued to escalate. And a taste. What wouldn't she give for just one taste of the throbbing male pulse she knew lay hidden right under the knot of the brown tie.

A slow warmth began working its way outward from her middle regions, tingling to her very fingertips, and Katherine jerked her mind back to their conversation.

"I was a commercial artist. Advertising."

Hunter pursed his full lips thoughtfully. "Advertising? That's definitely running in the fast lane," he murmured more to himself than to her. The gold in his eyes flickered with undeniable interest. "Quite a different life-style from the one you've got going for yourself now. Out here."

Katherine tried not to be irritated by the way he made Arizona sound like Timbuktu.

Hunter rubbed his jaw. "Was a man involved in this rather abrupt life-style change?"

"In a way."

Katherine asked herself why she was even discussing this with Hunter St. James. It was certainly none of his business. After tonight, she'd never see the man again. He'd return to New York, purchase *Spring Snow*, and that would be that.

She refilled the coffee mug, holding the pyrex glass pot up to him questioningly. Hunter shook his dark head, declining.

"I was married," she said. "To an up-and-coming young account executive. Rising Madison Avenue type, if you know what I mean?"

Hunter nodded. Of course he did, she thought. In the jungle atmosphere of New York City, it was survival of the fittest. And she knew instinctively, eyeing Hunter, that this was a man who'd always survive. Contemplating the dark, harshly hewn features honestly, Katherine had no doubt the man could be as ruthless as necessary. But whatever tactics he used, she also knew that dishonesty and fraud weren't his weapons.

"Anyway," she continued softly running a finger around the rim of the handmade earthenware mug, "Steven wanted, more than anything, to have his own agency. He'd been working with a major cosmetic account, which he hoped to use, along with a few smaller ones, to branch out on his own. The only fly in the ointment was, of course, that he needed some dynamite proposal to lure the account away."

"And he knew just the artist who could develop such a revolutionary concept. Free of charge." The dry tone indicated the story wasn't a new one to Hunter.

Katherine nodded, her mouth twisting in self-derision. "I spent every spare minute away from the office on the proposal. I knew it was underhanded, but Steven told me it was the way everyone did business in advertising. Eat or be eaten."

"To a point," he surprised her by blandly agreeing, "Steven wasn't far off. Did he capture the account with your work?"

Katherine nodded her dark glossy head. "He did. As well as the owner of the company. A wealthy, successful woman who had no end of important contacts. It seems," her throaty voice was laced with an old private bitterness, "I'd outlived my usefulness."

"So you tucked your tail between your legs and ran away."

"Well, I certainly couldn't stay on at the agency," she retorted hotly. "After all, I helped Steven steal a major account. And the newly established Steven Markson Agency wasn't hiring my type of artist."

"Your type?" He raised a dark brow inquiringly.

"Ex-wives. His new wife was the jealous type. I suppose she was astute enough to realize that if he was willing to have an affair with her, while married to me, he might be tempted to continue bad habits. But she made his tight leash more palatable by feeding him new business contacts. She was smart enough to see that success is Steven's first and only true love. Something I didn't catch on to until it was too late."

"How did you end up here?"

"I was shattered," Katherine admitted, surprising herself with her openness. It was easy to relate this to him. "Monica and I had gone to New York together after college. She'd come back here for a vacation and stayed. She convinced me that sunshine and tennis were just what I needed, and she was right. I managed to put myself back together, with a little help from my friend," she parodied the song lightly.

"And you did it so well, too." Hunter's amber eyes lit with approval as he took in the loose, ebony waves of her hair. In the morning sunlight, her raven-black hair was cast with shimmering indigo lights.

He unfolded his body from the chair, crossing the space between them. His arm resting lightly on her back, he led her over to the dining alcove, where he stood with her in front of the mirrored wall. His strong hands moved lightly through the clouds of loose, unbound hair, lifting it up to the sun's slanting yellow rays.

"Look at this hair," he murmured, touching a bit to his lips momentarily. "Midnight, unlit by a single star. Romantic, and as soft and glossy as spun silk. And those eyes"—his gaze met hers in the mirror, nodding encouragingly as her pupils widened, merging with the dark iris—"soft and gentle as a doe. I've never seen eyes that reveal so many secrets about a woman."

Hunter moved behind her, his hands reaching around to lightly trace up the high, slanted line of her cheekbone. "So, so delicate," he murmured, "a late-summer rose, in full bloom."

Hunter stared, transfixed at their image in the mirror and Katherine felt that strange jolt as their eyes met and caressed in the oddly familiar way. He was holding her so her back was pressed lightly against the firm wall of his chest, his thighs hard against the back of her legs. Katherine shivered slightly, wanting more.

Hunter, feeling the delicate tremor, turned her in the circle of his arms and his fingers laced together around her waist, holding her lightly, but not forcefully. His eyes traced the full line of her lips, and she waited, unable to move from his heated examination.

"And your lips," he murmured, desire making his voice rough and husky, "are as dark and sweet as mulled, warm wine. And every bit as heady an experience."

His lips moved closer, touching hers with a silky caress. Katherine felt a slow, warm tingle of pleasure work its way up her spine. Her hands moved to the hard, firm line of his shoulder, kneading at him with little clutchings in the buttery soft suede of his jacket.

"You're going to be too warm in that today," she whispered as his lips left hers to treat her face to a series of stinging, tantalizing kisses.

"I'm always too warm when I'm around you, sexy Kate," he growled. He touched his warm lips to the tip of her nose, his tongue flicking out lightly against her skin. Then he moved the kiss to her eyelid, where he brushed it gently, his touch as delicate as a newly fallen snowflake. Katherine waited, her eyes closed, her breath held in her lungs, for Hunter to treat her other eyelid to such a feathery, wonderful touch. But he seemed to have no definite order to the tender assault, moving instead to her temple.

She leaned into him, her legs growing weak as those enticing lips traced a line from the throbbing pulse at her temple, down the side of her face to taste the delicate line of her jaw. One strong hand left the light embrace that had been holding her to him and moved to the corner of her mouth, where his thumb played tenderly with her full, soft lips until he coaxed them slightly apart. Then, as her eyes opened, Katherine watched the dark lashes flutter on his harshly cut cheeks as his own eyes closed and the dark-brown head lowered to begin a slow exploration of her mouth.

Katherine felt a warmth invading her body that had nothing to do with the bright Arizona sun streaming into the sunny room. It flowed over her like warm, golden honey and she grew pliant in the strong arms that were caressing her back.

When she'd gotten up from that fitful sleep, Katherine had vowed not to permit this to happen today. He was only in Arizona to purchase *Spring Snow*, the portrait she'd completed after hundreds of false starts. She could never become seriously involved with him, she asserted as she brushed her teeth. Hunter was everything she studiously avoided in a man.

He was arrogant and unbending; Katherine preferred men she could move around to her own way of thinking. It was definitely preferable to be the one in control, she'd discovered, after having served for two years as a doormat to Steven. She was in no way unfeminine or domineering, but she was strong-willed. It was simply easier to date men who'd acquiesce to an independent, self-possessed woman.

And Hunter was definitely wound far too tightly for her personal taste. Katherine enjoyed the leisurely pace of the desert southwest. While she was more than willing to lock herself away for days at a time as she feverishly prepared for a showing or was excited about a particular subject, she also enjoyed the chance to linger poolside, soaking up the warm sunshine.

Hunter, on the other hand, appeared as if he

turned the switch to high from the moment he leaped from bed and kept it at full force, barreling his way through life. She could imagine him seated behind a broad mahogany desk, not one crisp dark hair out of place, fielding three telephone conversations at once, while six other lines blinked on hold. Hunter St. James not only loved the rat race, she decided, he was the leader of the pack.

As she dressed, Katherine also used their obvious difference in appearance as an argument against further involvement. Hunter hadn't emerged from the pages of *Dress for Success*, he'd surpassed it years ago. Spit-polished to a glossier shine than her stainless-steel kitchen appliances, right down to the tips of his Wall Street toes. Katherine, on the other hand, dressed up only for parties. As for shoes, she never wore them unless absolutely necessary. Even then she'd be more likely to be found in a soft, well-worn pair of sneakers than patent leather pumps. The extravagance of color she wore as matter of course appeared to be a whirling kaleidoscope next to the understated elegance of Hunter's conservatively hued wardrobe.

No, she'd decided before he'd arrived, after tonight she'd never see this man again. And although he'd leave with the rights to a painting it had taken her five years to complete, at least he'd be back in New York. Miles from Carefree, Arizona.

She'd told herself all that and more. But now, intimately entwined with him, her fingers splayed across his back under the suede jacket, Katherine was rapidly drifting under his persuasive spell once again.

"Let's forget the shopping trip," he murmured enticingly, his breath warm and seductive in the delicate convolutions of her ear.

"We can't," she argued softly, attempting rational thought over the dull roaring in her mind. "You can't go to the party dressed like this. No one will ever believe you're K. L. Michaels."

"Then we'll go later," he suggested as his hands slipped under her crimson top. The touch of his hand on the bare skin of her midriff stole the breath from her body.

"Hunter," she protested, "we've got a thousand things to do to get you ready for tonight." She mustered up every bit of her lingering strength to fight the damning skill of his seducing hands. "We'll go now."

"All right," he sighed. His hands returned from their warm haven and he tucked the material back into the waistband of her jeans. "Damn, but you are stubborn. And to think I only came west to track down a grizzled, old cowpoke who'd keep uping the ante until his western poker sense told him I'd reached my limit. That would've been a cinch compared to what you're making me do for that portrait."

"You know," she said conversationally as they made their way to the car, "I just realized I've never set a price on *Spring Snow*, because I never intended to sell it. I don't suppose you'd be willing to give me a hint as to your upper limit?"

She leaned against the door of her car, looking up into the amber eyes with a teasing, appealing expression. She knew that no experienced wheeler-dealer, as she perceived Hunter to be, would ever be foolhardy enough to disclose the price he was willing to pay for anything.

"No," he answered, just as she'd expected.

"I didn't think so." Katherine turned to put the key

in the lock. Hunter went around the other side of the car, settling his long frame into the passenger seat.

"Because I don't have a limit," he elaborated on his answer. "Whatever you decide, Kate, I'm willing to pay."

"You can't be serious," she gasped. Her hand had been moving to insert the key into the ignition, but it hit the steering column as her attention remained riveted on his inscrutable expression.

"Of course I am. I don't have the slightest idea what *Spring Snow* is worth, Kate. You do. Set a price and I'll meet it. See how simple that is?"

White teeth flashed in a wide crescent, but Katherine told herself that there hadn't been a single thing about this man that had been remotely simple thus far. And she had no reason to believe things would swerve from the status quo.

Chapter Four

"Are you saying that because of yesterday?" she asked softly, afraid of his answer. She didn't want special payment. It made her near surrender seem different. Cheap, somehow, and tawdry. Decidedly tawdry.

A dark brow climbed the jutting forehead. "Because I know how badly you and Monica need my help? Or because"—his tawny eyes took on a strange expression—"I wanted to make love to you? And still do."

Katherine had trouble forcing the words past the rapidly growing lump in her throat. "The second," she murmured, breaking free from the assessing gaze to stare out the windshield.

"Don't let that earthy, feminine appeal of yours go to your head, Kate," the deep voice taunted her lightly. "I've no doubt you're good, sweetheart. All signs so far point to that. But nobody's good enough to be given a blank check."

Katherine glared at him. "If you're always this complimentary when you're trying to get a woman into bed, Hunter," she accused sharply, anger serving to hide her pain, "you must go through a hell of a lot of women."

She twisted the key viciously in the ignition, gunning the engine as she backed out of the driveway. She threw the car into forward, the grinding of the gears deterring Hunter from commenting on her tautly flung reproach. He watched her warily instead, seemingly uneasy at the speed with which she hurled the car around the tight curves of the winding mountain road.

"I asked you to set a price," he commented finally in a low, neutral tone. Her anger had dissipated somewhat and her driving had become more prudent. "Because I don't know a single thing about western art prices. I'm trusting you to be fair."

Katherine's foot almost slammed the brake through the floor at his casual words. Instead, she struggled for control and pulled the car into the first wide spot on the narrow hillside road. Resting her forearms on the top of the steering wheel, she lowered her head to them for a long, silent moment. Then she turned, her cheek against the padded wheel.

"You don't know *anything* about the prices of western art?"

He shook his dark head. "No. Although from the looks of your house, it's not cheap. You didn't buy that place and all that furniture, as uncomfortable as the stuff is, with trading stamps."

A chill settled in the pit of her stomach. "If you don't know anything about prices, then I suppose you don't know anything about western art." There was a plaintive sound to her thin voice and Hunter smiled apologetically at the plea in it.

"Nope. Not a thing. I'm sorry," he added, as if it might help matters.

He was sorry. Katherine felt as if she'd just been kicked by a horse. And from the pain, it must have been a Clydesdale. Did he think that being sorry would do any good?

"I'd assumed that you were familiar with the art." She turned flashing eyes accusingly on him, hating him for spoiling everything.

"Hey!" Hunter held up a hand as if to ward off her building fury. "I never said that. All I ever said was that I was here to buy *Spring Snow*."

"Why in the world would you want to buy that damn painting if you didn't collect western art?" Her voice rose shrilly, ricocheting about them in the confines of the car.

Hunter looked at her as if she were crazy. Which I am, she thought wildly. The man is driving me insane! Twenty-four hours ago, Katherine Michaels' life had been perfect. Now look at it!

"I told you that it was personal," he said with gentle censure. "I'm prepared to reveal those reasons when—and only when—I feel the time is right. For now, all you need to know is that I want that painting and I'm willing to pay whatever price is necessary. Including going through with this ridiculous little charade you've cooked up."

His low, measured tones took some of the wind from her sails and Katherine rubbed her forehead with her fingertips, attempting to soothe away the headache that was threatening behind her eyes.

"All right," she agreed reluctantly. "So what do you suggest we do now?"

She watched the fine network of lines deepen slightly at the corner of his smiling eyes. "You can give me a crash course this afternoon," he suggested. "Enough to be able to carry on a conversation with Monica's sheikh, anyway. I'm not exactly thickheaded, Kate." Hunter granted her an encouraging chuckle.

"Surely you can teach me enough to get by. If we get into trouble, we'll simply pen some crib notes onto my shirt cuffs."

Katherine smiled, in spite of her lingering doubt, and dropped her eyes to the creamy silk. "You, Hunter St. James, allowing anyone to scribble on those immaculate clothes?"

"Ah, but they'll be your clothes, remember? You're paying," he reminded her. "So, sweetheart, you're the one who can worry about stain remover."

"It's worth a try," she muttered, restarting the car and continuing down the hill. "At any rate, it's the only chance we've got."

"Don't worry," Hunter promised, "I wouldn't have agreed to do it if I thought I'd end up sounding like a fool. It's going to be bad enough looking like one."

Her dark eyes slid down the long, lean lines of the body sitting next to her. "You'll look fine," she promised. "Just fine."

More than fine, she decided later, the man looked terrific! The blue denim of the jeans shaped his legs, the soft material stretched tautly over the muscles of his thighs. The yoked shirt strained across a powerful chest and outlined the hard ridge of his wide shoulders. Hunter walked toward her from the dressing room with a lazy insolence, the predatory gracefulness of the stride not revealing for an instant that the wedge-heeled boots were not his usual footwear.

"Well?" He stood before her, a challenge in his spread-legged stance and fisted hands resting on slim hips.

"You look fine," she said with understated calm, trying to find a spot of his solid figure that wouldn't affect her so devastatingly. "But you need a tie."

"I have ties."

"You have silk stockbroker ties," she argued firmly. "What you need is a bolo tie." Her eyes drifted from the muscled ridge of his chest up to the triangle of dark hair visible at the open neck of the cotton shirt. Once again she had that strange, sudden urge to press her lips to that warm, tanned spot. Instead, she reached blindly for a tie on the display rack, picking up a corded one with metal tips. The slide clasp was a triangle of jet-shot turquoise set in silver.

"This will be fine."

"It looks like two shoelaces," he argued, eyeing it skeptically.

"Don't be silly." Katherine overrode him with the air of a woman fully used to getting her own way. "Everyone out here wears them. Even my banker," she stressed.

Hunter arched a disbelieving dark brow.

"It's true," she insisted, still holding it out to him between her fingers. "His has a slide made of clear Lucite with a scorpion inside. Which, from the rate of interest the man charges, is perfectly appropriate."

"Do I have to wear it? I don't wear jewelry."

"It's not jewelry," Katherine argued softly, growing a bit impatient. "And look," she tried another tactic, "it matches your belt."

"I'm not wild about the belt either," he muttered, a brief shadow of irritation darkening his eyes as he looked down at the tooled-leather belt with a wide silver-and-turquoise buckle.

"Hunter, if I'm paying for all this, I think I should be the one entitled to pick it out," Katherine snapped waspishly, losing her patience.

"All right." A devilish gleam suddenly brightened

the golden-amber eyes. "Put it on me and we'll see what it looks like."

Put her arms up around that strong, bronzed neck? He had to think her a complete idiot. No way would she take a chance like that with those wicked lights dancing in his beautiful, inviting eyes.

"You're a big boy, Hunter. Put it on yourself."

He remained steadfast. "You're buying it, you put it on," he instructed. "And count yourself damn lucky, woman, that I didn't make you dress me completely. I could have, you know."

"I never would have done that."

A taunting ghost of a smile played across the full lips. "You would if I'd insisted," he contradicted. "Just because I'm letting you boss me around like this in public, sweet Kate, doesn't mean I'm always going to permit you to get away with it. As it is," the seductively low-pitched note was a barely concealed threat, "you'll pay for this little display of high-handedness."

"I haven't been any such thing," she hissed at him, her dark eyes circling the room to see if their altercation was being observed. "And, even if I had been, you couldn't do a single thing about it."

"I think after we leave here, you should let me buy you something for the party tonight," he suggested suddenly, throwing her entirely off her heated track.

"What?" Katherine blinked like a confused owl, as she attempted to make sense of the swift detour their conversation had just taken.

She gasped as his head swooped down and he planted a quick kiss upon her opened lips.

"I'd like to buy you a pretty party dress." He laughed. "Something ruffly and feminine. Because it's high time, my shrewish Kate, that you learned just who wears the pants in this relationship."

His tawny, teasing gaze ran down the length of her body.

Katherine could feel her teeth grinding and she bit her full bottom lip to keep from shouting obscenities in front of the sales clerks. But her black eyes were shooting daggers directly into smiling gold ones.

"You don't need to try it." She closed her fist around the bolo tie and, spinning on her heels, marched toward the counter. She glared back at Hunter over her shoulder.

"Well, are you coming?"

The devastating eyes were awash with laughter. "Yes, dear," he answered, following on her heels like an obedient puppy.

Hunter remained at his best behavior the remainder of the day, giving Katherine the eerie feeling she'd been handed a grenade with the pin already pulled. The question was not *if* the damn thing would explode, but *when*.

They ate lunch at a restaurant built on a floating dock extending over a manmade, sparkling blue lake. As the water slapped lightly against the pilings underneath them, they discussed western art over crab-and-avocado salads.

They continued the lectures while she drove back up to her house, this time taking the hairpin turns with more caution. And the tutoring continued for three more hours while they sat in her courtyard garden. Then she leaned back in the wrought-iron chair, a tulip-shaped glass of chilled white wine in her hand. "Final-exam time."

She unceasingly flashed paintings from a pile of catalogs like a teacher drilling a student in multiplication tables. When she was done, Katherine finally allowed herself a smile. This just might work. She lifted her glass to him in a salute.

"I think you'll pass," she said with a note of relief in her voice.

"I told you I could do it." Hunter flipped through the stacks of catalogs she'd spread out on the table between them. "You know this stuff isn't half-bad. I was expecting something far more . . ."

"Hokey?" she asked, her lips curving slightly.

He had the grace to look embarrassed. "I suppose that's the word I was looking for."

"As far as hokey goes," Katherine enlightened him, "the paintings these days manage to blend a romanticized vision of the West with a historically accurate portrayal of the way of life. An anthropologist studying a painting could tell which tribe the Indians belonged to by the feathers in their war bonnets, the loincloths, or the types of ponies they're riding. These paintings reflect values a lot of people share, Hunter; optimism, individualism, the strength of overcoming hardships. There's plenty of room for expression in the arts. Some people like their art to have a solid base in reality." She grinned self-consciously. "School's out. End of lecture."

Instead of the teasing laughter she'd expected to find in his face at her emotional defense of western art, Katherine was surprised to find him studying her face intently.

"Did you always feel this way?"

Katherine shook her head, remembering the first time she'd eaten with Monica in a steak house. She'd made fun of the oil paintings lining the white adobe walls.

"No. When I wasn't doing advertising work, I

preferred impressionism. Peaceful, misty, ethereal scenes."

"Quite a change," he noted, pouring them each a little more wine from the tall carafe.

"When I got hit with a jolt of realism in my own life," she confessed, "it seemed to spill over into my work. I like the honesty of western art. It matches who I am today."

"And tomorrow?"

She shrugged, a graceful gesture. "I don't know," she admitted. "I like taking my life one day at a time. Steven and I shared so many plans, and look what happened to them. No"—she smiled softly—"I'll face tomorrow when it comes." She glanced down at her watch. "It's time for you to get back to the inn, Hunter."

He rose instantly, towering over her. "What time do you want me back, professor?"

"Let's not push our luck," Katherine considered thoughtfully. "Monica's parties always start late. Hopefully, we'll be able to put in a quick appearance and take off. Let's make it around nine."

"It's nice to know you're so anxious to spend an evening with me," he remarked. "You've no idea what that does for my ego."

As if anything could deflate that masculine ego, she thought. It was as firm and rock-hard as the body in which it thrived.

"Now, don't be difficult," she coaxed him. "I've spent the entire day with you."

"You have," he allowed promptly. "And may I point out that we've gotten along admirably?"

"For oil and water," Katherine pointed out.

Hunter bent, placing his glass on the table next to the glossy, colorful catalogs. Deliberately, he reached out and took her glass from her hands, placing it next to his. Then he brought her out of her chair into an intimate embrace.

"Oil and flame," he murmured in correction. His golden eyes sensually explored her face as knuckles brushed along her cheekbone, leaving a scattering of sparks on her skin.

The hand trailed down her throat, halting any protest that might be gathering there, attempting to work its way to her lips. Katherine could feel a warm glow working its way through her blood, and her hands, of their own volition, moved to circle his waist. She clung to him weakly, awaiting the devastation of her senses she knew would come with a mere kiss.

Hunter's lips lightly grazed her mouth with sweet familiarity and she bent like a willow in supplication to the wind. But with a deep sigh he backed away, the kiss ending far too circumspectly for her own growing desire.

"Oil and flame." A half-smile played about his mouth, full of masculine self-satisfaction. He'd taken off his jacket in the warm heat of the afternoon sun and now he picked it up from the back of the chair, holding it on one finger over his shoulder.

"Hunter?"

He turned in the doorway, eyeing her over his shoulder. "Yes, Kate?"

"Why are you being so agreeable all of a sudden?"

"All of a sudden?" He raised an eyebrow quizzically.

Katherine's slim hands made a slight, helpless gesture. "You've been a model of cooperation all afternoon. Even now, when I asked you to leave . . ." Her voice drifted off as a deep, telling crimson entered her cheeks.

There was a flicker of interest in his hooded amber

eyes, then they lit with sparks of humor. His lips curved into a bold grin as he lounged his long length against the door, eyeing her with genuine amusement.

"Wishing I'd stay and help you dress?"

The deep mocking voice was definitely provocative and Katherine lashed out at herself for opening Pandora's box. Why couldn't she have left well enough alone? The man had been cooperating, for heaven's sake!

"Of course not! But you did threaten me in the clothing store."

A look of sheer innocence appeared on his rough features, ill-suited for the craggy face. "Me? Threaten you? Are you sure you've got the right man, Kate? My mother taught me never to threaten a lady."

"Did she also teach you to lie so well, Hunter?"

The grooves on either side of his mouth deepened and he grinned wolfishly. "No. I taught myself to do that."

Giving her a jaunty little salute, he left her looking wildly around the garden for something to throw. The hardbound gallery catalog hit the door frame moments after his dark head had already cleared the space.

In a vain attempt to cool down, Katherine turned to her painting. The deep concentration required by her craft never ceased to serve as a balm to stretched and sensitive nerves, and Hunter's presence these past two days had left them in tatters.

Not only had the man insinuated himself into her life, he'd taken control of her subconscious too, she discovered as she filled in the details of the painting. It should have been a safe-enough subject—a cowboy seated by a campfire, warming his hands on a dented, metal mug—but, Katherine would know those long fingers anywhere. They'd already proven their ability to create an undeniable yearning deep within her. The cowboy's eyes were a brilliant tawny gold, observing her from the three-foot canvas with a mocking, knowing gleam. This was not an exhausted, cold and hungry man, stopping for a brief respite from early spring roundup. This was a man with seduction on his mind. Ridiculous!

She tried to ignore the inviting eyes, planning to change them after the paint dried. Her brush moved in rapid, sure strokes as she filled in the ruffled hair, which was exposed to the harshly driven snow. The short burnt umber was too closely clipped for any cowboy, and not at all the dark-bark color she'd first intended as a contrast to the gray and white swirling flakes.

Grinding her teeth, Katherine covered the crisp russet hair with a rumpled weathered stetson. As a last retaliatory measure, her brush moved rapidly over the canvas, tossing heavy splotches of thick mud onto the man's long duster.

"There," she mumbled, "see how you like that, Hunter." The idea of him covered with the reddish wet clay mud like that amused her until she faced the obvious fact that she had, indeed, painted a likeness of Hunter St. James. The harsh rugged lines of the cowboy's face didn't even remotely resemble the eighteen-year-old boy she'd originally sketched in.

Irrationally furious at him for creating this confusion of mind, Katherine covered the painting with two bold cross slashes of black before giving up on any further attempt to work today.

"I cheated."

Katherine's mouth dropped open as she stood in the doorway, staring up at Hunter. At least she suspected it was him. But if she had thought the clothes she'd purchased had revealed a more honest version of Hunter St. James, the dark vision filling her doorway had to be a stranger.

She could only continue to stare dumbly, stunned by the transformation. Before, when clad in the conservative, formal clothing, Hunter had possessed a hint of steel, an unbending, compelling arrogance. His masculinity had only been enhanced by the western shirt and jeans he'd worn this afternoon in the store.

But now ... Dear Lord, what had she done? Katherine felt as if she'd been given a huge block of marble and, like a master sculptor, had managed to free the true spirit locked within the icy stone.

This man was too rawly masculine, a law unto himself. Hunter oozed a self-confidence and ruthlessness that boded ill to any poor soul who might be crazy enough to test his authority. As he stood before her, exhibiting that lean, muscular body for her approval, she could feel her heart pounding wildly against her rib cage. Katherine had the uneasy feeling she knew precisely how Dr. Frankenstein felt when his monster had broken loose.

This man had nothing to do with peace or calm. He exuded fire and passion. And sheer, unadulterated danger.

"Those aren't the clothes I bought!"

Wide shoulders shrugged in a gesture of dismissal as he supported himself with one hand against the door frame, looking down at her.

"I felt like an extra in an old Gene Autry movie," Hunter complained. "I knew you couldn't stand me wearing a suit, and I sure as hell couldn't take the way I looked after the make-over. So, I compromised." He spread his hands out, palms upward. "Take me or leave me, Kate."

I'll take you, some passionate part of her brain screeched out. Fortunately, the thought was censored by her more self-protective mind before she'd blurted it out loud. Hunter was clad all in black. He'd cast aside the jeans, shirt, and flamboyant buckle and bolo tie. Ebony boots glistened from beneath the slightly flared pants and a black stetson was pulled down slightly over his golden-amber eyes.

Those eyes were glinting at her amazed appraisal with a knowing, sensual glance. Katherine felt a deep relief flooding over her as her sense of humor came to the forefront to salvage her stunned senses.

"That's what I did wrong. I forgot the hat. Otherwise, you'd have been perfect."

"It's just as well you forgot it, then," he murmured, his hands reaching out to rest in light possession on either side of her waist. "Because I'm content to leave perfection to my lady."

His thumbs were lightly rubbing the silk of her dress, his eyes reflecting the brilliancy of the material and something far more basic. Katherine had found herself dressing for him tonight, realizing it as she'd tried on and discarded almost the entire contents of her closet. The final choice had been the silk dress with colors ranging from a bright scarlet, through cherry, to a deep cyclamen pink as it swirled across the fabric. The hues were a perfect foil for her vibrant coloring, giving her all the exotic brilliance of a hot-house flower.

Katherine remained framed in the doorway, submitting herself to his prolonged study, secure in the knowledge that she looked every bit as elegant as any of his New York women.

Her hair was brushed back from her forehead, as sleek and glossy as raven's wings, a dark cloud tumbling in confusion over her bare shoulders. Her wide dark eyes held the richness of velvet and were sumptuously fringed as they lifted to meet Hunter's. And, although Katherine knew she was playing with fire, her cherry-red lips curved in a smile ripe with invitation.

"You can invite me in," Hunter's deep voice rumbled, "or take a chance on scandalizing your neighbors with the kiss I'm about to give you."

Katherine's eyelids fluttered exaggeratedly. "That bad?"

"Or that good. Depending on how you look at it." There was a glint of pleasant lust in his amber eyes that sent a flurry of emotion coursing through her body.

This is only a physical attraction, she reminded herself firmly as she stepped aside, inviting him silently into the room. Only physical, she repeated as he shut the door with a backward kick, not taking his smoldering gaze from her warm, welcoming one. Nothing more, she stressed, eagerly capitulating to his demands as he propelled her hips into his.

Hunter's lips were fierce as they molded her mouth, the abrasive, flicking tongue evoking a warmth in her thighs. His strong hands ran from her hips to her breasts, augmenting the ravenous message of his mouth, and Katherine felt as if he'd lit a fire between their bodies. It was as if the flames had seared away their clothing and she could feel her nipples responding to the touch of his hard chest against them.

Katherine arched in instinctive response and her fingers twisted convulsively through his crisp dark hair, the black stetson falling to the hand-painted tile unnoticed. She was dissolving in his arms and she realized, through her ignited senses, that the soft, desperate moans were coming from her own ravaged lips.

"Oh, Kate," he groaned, his heated breath filling her mouth with its sweetness, "you pick the damnedest times to pull out the stops."

His hands had slid under the full, filmy silk, moving up her nylon-clad thigh. Katherine gasped as they moved inside the waistband of her panty hose, reaching to clutch her rounded buttocks, kneading her flesh.

"I know," she sighed, turning her lips into his throat, tasting his warm, moist skin. "I just can't think straight when you're around, Hunter. It'll be a relief when you're gone."

Katherine felt him stiffen against her for a long, horribly silent moment, then the hands left the warmth of her body and straightened her disheveled clothing. When she dared to glance up into his face, those warm amber eyes had hardened to agate.

"Hunter?" It was a whisper as she placed her nails on his black sleeve. Blood, she thought absently, staring at the contrasting colors. It looked as if she'd drawn blood. And God knows, he was suddenly acting as if he were wounded.

"A relief? Really, Kate?"

Her hand pressed against the black wall of his chest and she could feel the increased tempo of his heartbeat under her palm.

"I don't know," she murmured honestly. "You've really confused me, Hunter. To tell you the truth, I don't think I've thought or acted like myself from the moment I saw you at the post office. I don't understand any of it."

"Don't think about it, honey," he advised, the harsh features softening somewhat. "Just go with what you feel for now. There'll be plenty of time to figure it out later."

Later? When he was gone? Perhaps he was right. Once they'd gone their separate ways, all this could be put into perspective. After all, wasn't she the one who'd decided to live one day at a time?

"All right, Hunter," Katherine answered him softly, her fingers combing his dark hair back into order. "But"—she smiled up into his eyes—"if I go with everything I feel, we'll never get to that party. And Monica will be out half a million dollars."

He laughed, a deep rumbling sound, enjoying her honesty. "That would probably be the most expensive roll in the hay in history," he agreed, his fingers lifting the soft clouds of dark hair and allowing them to drift over her shoulders.

"Come on, sweetheart," he instructed, dropping a quick kiss to her neck. "Duty calls. It's time for K. L. Michaels to put in an appearance."

Chapter Five

"Darlings!" Monica swept Katherine up into a warm embrace, the flowing gold-and-silver chiffon sleeves of her gown spreading like the wings of a metallic butterfly. "I've been going absolutely mad worrying about you two," she hissed into her friend's ear. "What kept you?"

Monica backed away a bit and green eyes searched Katherine's face, which was still softened with her earlier, tumultuous emotions. At the query, a warm flush had slowly crept into the already rosy cheeks.

"Oh. Well, under the circumstances," Monica allowed, on a note of musical laughter, "I appreciate the effort even more."

She turned her bright, knowing gaze on Hunter. "Absolutely breathtaking," she announced, the emerald gaze not missing an inch as they roved from the brim of the black stetson right down to the glossy polished black boots. "I can see why Katherine was in no hurry to share her snowbird with the rest of us."

"Then I pass?" Hunter inquired dryly, his eyes spiked with good nature.

"Honey," she said as she slipped her arm through

his and led him into the crowded room, "you not only pass, you set the standard."

Katherine was left to follow as Hunter was swept off. An odd sensation pricked her heart as she watched Monica chatter gaily up into Hunter's obviously amused face. For heaven's sake, she scolded herself firmly, she's your best friend, and she's in trouble. So be generous! A little voice in the far reaches of her mind agreed that generosity was all very nice, but she still wished Monica would take her hands off Hunter St. James.

Monica was leading him to a man whose onyx eyes watched their approach with the intensity of a hungry eagle. The flowing robes, Katherine decided, were worn as much for his image as for comfort. He was taller than she'd imagined, and possessed a great presence. But the semi-circle of stern-faced men dressed in dark suits were even larger. Mountains. They could have easily made up the defensive line of any NFL team in the nation. It was obvious their sole responsibility in life was the protection of their sheikh.

Katherine told herself it should come as no surprise that Hunter wouldn't be intimidated by the silent group of dark men. Or that he'd betray any nervousness. Katherine, on the other hand, could feel her palms moistening, and she wiped them surreptitiously on the flaming silk of her dress. She'd come up behind them just as Monica had concluded with the introductions and flitted away, like the coward she was. Katherine knew exactly how her friend felt. She herself would love to hide in a corner and await the fatal outcome of this little meeting, but she felt it her duty to stand by in case Hunter needed some help.

The black eyes slid immediately from Hunter's

craggy face to hers, darkening as the sheikh examined her with sheer male approval. A look that needed no translation. "Ah, Mr. Michaels," his heavily accented voice addressed Hunter, "Monica neglected to introduce me to your charming friend."

Hunter turned. His face was surprisingly neutral, but his amber eyes smiled encouragement. Long fingers slipped about her waist as he pulled her to him possessively.

"Sheikh Ahmed Fahd Rasid al-Tajir," his tongue slid easily over the long, difficult name, "may I present my fiancée, Katherine St. James."

Katherine's mind was still protesting the easy way he'd claimed a relationship they certainly didn't have, when the name he'd given her came crashing down around her ears. Her dark eyes flew up to an impossibly bland face.

The sheikh's face fell visibly, but he nodded at Katherine, his tone polite and correctly proper.

"You are a most fortunate man, Mr. Michaels. I know you Americans are permitted only one wife. Up until now I'd always considered that an unhappy misfortune for the American male. However"—broad white teeth flashed under the black mustache—"with Miss St. James as a betrothed, I believe a man might very well survive the constraints of monogamy."

"Thank you," Hunter acknowledged, infuriating Katherine by treating her like a prized show animal. "I have no doubt she'll prove most satisfactory."

His fingers were caressing her skin under the soft silk and it was all Katherine could do to keep from stamping her thin spiked heel directly on his foot.

Fiancée indeed! Satisfactory, was she? Where did he get off with remarks like that? She couldn't even protest the manner in which he'd so cavalierly given her his name. Not without blowing the entire scheme.

"I hear you've found my paintings to your liking," Hunter addressed the tall, swarthy man. "I'm honored." The smooth tones sounded completely sincere.

"I have fallen in love with your American West," the rumbling voice confessed. "I came here hoping to find the cowboys and Indians riding down your street, but Monica tells me that is no longer the way of things." His face reflected his obvious disappointment.

"That's true," Katherine answered, drawing the surprised stare of the sheikh. He seemed shocked that she would dare to enter so readily into the men's conversation.

"Not entirely true, darling." Hunter's smooth, deep tones overrode her with a look at the sheikh that suggested, Women what can you do with them? "There's a rodeo next week. I imagine you'd be able to see your share of the wild West in action there."

The dark face brightened visibly and Katherine shot Hunter a withering glance. "I'm sure that Sheikh al-Tajir's schedule is far too busy to allow him to remain in Carefree for a silly little rodeo," she protested.

"Why, dear," Hunter's voice was smooth as silk, "surely you've heard that some of our most famous cowboys will be participating? Not to mention the delegations from most of the western Indian tribes. No"—he shook his dark head—"this is no little rodeo. Three days, I believe it lasts? With a huge parade. Including," he sweetened the pot, "a group representing the Arizona Arabian Horse Owners Association."

"Arabians? As well as cowboys and Indians?" There

was a look of sheer bliss on the dark face, and a murmur of approval hummed through his entourage.

"Dear, I'm sure three days watching men ride horses around a dusty arena would be quite boring for such a well-traveled man as the sheikh." Her hand covered the large one resting on her hip and her fingers squeezed as hard as possible.

Katherine was forced to clench her jaws as he returned the gesture, crushing her hand with his male strength. It was an effort to keep the smile pasted on her face, but she did her best.

"I'm certain, dear," he murmured, seemingly unconscious of the pain he was causing, "that the sheikh is able to recognize this as the opportunity of a lifetime. As a devotee of our American West, he certainly wouldn't want to pass it up."

"You're right, of course," the booming, accented voice agreed instantly. He lifted his head, bright eyes searching the room. "Aha! Monica, my dear," he called out, waving an arm in her direction.

She'd been standing in a corner, jade eyes surveying the little scene nervously. She appeared at his side instantly, almost as if he'd conjured her up by rubbing a magic lamp.

"Good news," the sheikh said, black eyes as bright as a pair of jet buttons. "Mr. Michaels informs me there's to be a rodeo next week."

"Yes," she agreed, her worried gaze sliding briefly to Katherine's pale, tight features before returning to her guest's. "It's an annual event."

"You failed to tell me of this." A thick finger wagged.

Emerald eyes widened as her fingers twisted at a lock of flowing red hair. "I'm sorry, Ahmed, I suppose I was so caught up in my enthusiasm for our plans for the ballet, I forgot. Forgive me?"

There was a soft, beseeching tone in the throaty voice and he laughed, a great booming sound of a man enjoying himself.

"When you look at me with those soft jade eyes," he said with a note of male indulgence, "how can I not forgive my little desert flower? Especially now that I'll be here to see the debut of our joint venture. Because I'm staying for this rodeo!" He rubbed his hands together with the obvious glee of a child who's just been informed that he's going to the circus.

Katherine felt her heart crumble and fall around her feet. She used every bit of inner strength to stifle her sharp intake of alarm.

"And you and I shall attend this rodeo together, eh, my friend Michaels?"

The remainder of the party was a blur and Katherine moved as if in a trance. She was vaguely aware that drinks were being pressed into her numbed fingers, and she remembered Hunter encouraging food past her frozen lips, but that was all.

Hunter, on the other hand, seemed perfectly at ease discussing western art with the sheikh and a slow, building flame burned within her as he took credit for every painting she'd ever done. He was charmingly modest the whole time, and the nicer he was, the more Katherine wanted to dump the crystal punch bowl over the top of his head.

She pressed against the door of his rented sedan as he drove back to her house. She refused to utter a single word and the atmosphere building up in the interior of the car could've rivaled the worst Siberian winter.

"I think it went quite well," Hunter finally said

into the frozen silence. "All things considered."

Katherine stared out into the darkness, refusing to acknowledge his statement. As soon as he stopped the car, she jumped out. She desperately wanted to slam the door in his face, but she realized some thanks were in order. He'd helped her out of a tight jam. Then again, he'd also gotten her into a worse one, Katherine reminded herself, and she was entitled to keep her fury at full blast.

Monica had been exuberant enough for both of them as she'd floated with Hunter out to the car. His finely chiseled cheek still bore the poppy-red imprint of those thankful lips. So did the corner of his mouth.

"Thank you, Hunter. I know Monica appreciated your effort on her behalf. As I did." Katherine closed the door, pulling her shawl more firmly about her trembling shoulders as she headed toward the front door, head held high.

She didn't look back, but from the sound of the metal door slamming and the harsh click of the wedge-heeled boots upon her brick walk, she knew she wasn't going to get away with it this easily. Long fingers bit into the soft flesh of her shoulders, spinning her around to face him.

"All right." Hunter glowered down at her, topaz eyes sparkling with angry flames. "What in the hell is the matter with you?"

"Nothing," she answered, and tried to break free of his tight embrace, but his fingers dug in more firmly. "Hunter, you're hurting me," she complained, dark eyes accusing as they looked up into his puzzled frown.

"It's just the beginning," he threatened. "I want to know why the hell you're acting as if I'm Typhoid Mary."

"Let me go," she hissed up at the dark thundercloud of his face.

"Not until we get this settled."

Katherine glanced down wildly at their feet, once again wanting to stamp her high, sharp heel into his instep.

"I wouldn't try it if I were you," the low, threatening voice whispered in her ear. "Because I'd only give it right back. And I don't think those strappy little sandals would offer much protection."

"There are other ways," she threatened, her eyes locking with his, black obsidian cutting away at the equally hard agate. "I've taken self-defense training, Hunter."

"If that lovely knee even begins to move, darling, you'll find yourself flat on your back with me right on top of you. Ditto if you're fool enough to believe that any of those silly little judo throws you may have learned are capable of flipping me onto those bricks. And, if you slap me, it'd only serve to irritate the hell out of me. I'd probably slap you right back."

"You are no gentleman, Hunter St. James!"

"I never claimed to be." His hand moved, rubbing sensuous circles on her midriff. "There's only one method you could use to get me onto my back, sweet Kate. Why don't you try a little sugar for a change?"

His voice was black velvet, smothering her like a cashmere blanket, and Katherine fought against the unfathomable sensation. She couldn't—wouldn't—allow him to get away with it so easily.

"I'm furious with you for so many reasons, Hunter, I wouldn't even know where to start." Her fists rested on silken hips.

"Try the beginning," he suggested with a lazy, arrogant drawl.

"All right." Katherine faced him head on, a contemptuous, defiant lift to her chin. "First of all, you had the unmitigated gall to refer to me, in public, as your fiancée!"

"Excuse me." Hunter put a wealth of sarcasm into the deep tones. "I suppose I should've introduced you as my lover?"

"You didn't have to introduce me as anything! Not your lover or your fiancée! There was no reason to insinuate to the sheikh we have *any* type of relationship."

"The hell there wasn't! The bastard was looking at you as if you'd just won a spot in his goddamn harem. For your friend's sake, I didn't deck the guy. But I won't permit him to undress you with those beady black eyes right in front of me."

Her legs almost buckled under her at his fiercely possessive tone, and for a split second Katherine was grateful for the strong fingers digging into her shoulders; without them, she was certain she'd crumble to the brick walk.

Scorching heat burned her cheeks as she drew breath for a new attack. "And your name! You had the nerve to introduce me with your name."

She glared up into his face, meeting only a tight, challenging smile. "The name just slipped out. Besides," his voice was infuriatingly patronizing, "if I recall, you'd already insisted I take yours. I suddenly realized we'd never come up with a last name for you." A wicked, insinuating grin teased her. "I could've introduced you as Katherine Michaels. Then we could have told the sheikh you were my wife."

The long dark fingers massaged her bruised skin and Katherine jerked away from the light intimate embrace. He was attempting to end the argument and she glared at him, an arch-backed cat facing an aggressive dog.

"You're nothing to me. Do you understand that, Hunter? Nothing but a partner in a necessary business deal. That's all! And don't worry about your payoff. I'll call the gallery first thing in the morning."

She spun on her heel, unable to take any more of the confrontation. Jerking the door open with a twist of her key, she slipped quickly inside to slam it.

"Oh, no, you don't." Hunter put a wide black shoulder against it, pushing it open as if it were made of a pile of drifted feathers instead of solid mahogany. He moved into her entryway, and his arms encircled her waist like bands of forged steel, holding her helplessly to his long, intense study.

"You're dead wrong, Kate. We do have a relationship. Even if you don't want to admit it to any stupid Arab sheikh, you'd better start facing it yourself."

Anger, she reminded herself as one of Hunter's hands worked its treacherous magic against her rib cage and the other danced along the fine, delicate bones of her back. I'm furious with him. He's arrogant, demanding, and he practically begged Monica's damn sheikh to stay in town another week.

"That's another thing," she protested, her voice betraying the emotional struggle she was going through. An unruly being lurked inside her, wanting only to give up to the warm sensations those devastating hands of his were creating.

"What's another thing, honey?" She fought the hypnotism of his eyes as they brimmed with a lazy heat. It was warmth that no longer portrayed his anger, but something far more primitive.

"You told him about the rodeo and now he's staying. What are we going to do?"

"We, as in you and I?" Hunter gave her a look she could've poured on a waffle and her mind was scrambling in a last-ditch attempt to thwart him.

"No. We, as in Monica and I. You're going to be back in New York."

"Am I?" The dangerous fingers slid under the silk spaghetti strap, sliding it down off her shoulder. His dark head ducked to feather his lips across her soft satiny skin.

"Hunter. Please don't do that." Katherine pulled the strap back up, only to have her hand covered by his larger one.

The anger had completely vanished from his eyes. They only smoldered with undisguised desire, encouraging her to drown in their molten depths.

"No, Kate, I won't stop. Because we both know this is what you really want." The strap once again slid down her arm, followed in an instant by the one on her other slim shoulder.

"Hunter, I don't know that at all."

His chin rested on her dark ebony hair, his warm breath fanning the soft strands lightly. "Yes, Kate. It's right. Trust me."

Katherine tried to stifle a gasp as he tugged on the crimson silk, allowing his palms to cup her swelling breasts. Hunter, with all the instincts of a natural predator, hadn't missed the quick breath.

"I'm not going to let you send me back to that lonely inn when we can be spending the night in each other's arms. That's where we belong, Kate."

His touch was intoxicating, sending desire through Katherine's blood with the effervescence of sparkling dry champagne. Her hands ceased their pushing motion against his chest and began moving in delicate little circles instead.

"Hunter, this is all too soon."

"How can you say that?" he protested huskily. "Too soon for me to want you? I knew the moment I saw you that I had to have you, Kate. You and the painting. It's impossible to separate the two."

"We shouldn't," she murmured, her eyes closed to the stinging kisses he was scattering across her tender lids. "This is so foolish. Nothing can ever come of it."

His fingers lowered the zipper at the back of her dress, then his hands moved against the bared skin in erotic patterns, heating her flesh with a burning flame.

"You'll see it's right. You'll see, darling." Before she could say a word, he scooped her up into his steely arms and was striding down the hall with long, purposeful steps. His gold eyes searched every doorway they passed, bursting into searing flames as he finally located the proper one at the end of the hall. It was a huge sitting-room affair, her brass bed located on a two-step platform in an alcove at one end. Katherine closed her eyes momentarily, expecting to be tossed onto the mattress. But instead, Hunter sat down, taking her with him as he stretched out his full length.

"Hunter, this has got to stop."

"It can't, Kate. Don't you see that? There's no reason to deny ourselves. I want you. And I know you want me. We're not kids, honey. There's not a reason in the world why we shouldn't make each other happy."

Every increasingly intimate touch was causing Katherine's blood to boil with a wild, pagan beat and she tried one more time to bank the smoldering embers threatening to burst into new flame and engulf them both.

"You're mistaken, Hunter," she protested, not meaning a single word. "You're taking too much for granted."

His gaze moved across her wide forehead, her high cheekbones, caressing her doe-soft brown eyes before lingering on her full lips. He touched them briefly with his own, then his lips plucked lightly at her, his tongue tracing the full-blown outline, intoxicatingly teasing the corners.

"Open your lips," he instructed softly, his breath whispering against her soft skin. "I want to taste you, my sweet Kate."

Her lips parted at the slight pressure of his tantalizing tongue and it slipped inside, searching out the hidden corners of her mouth with tender exploration. Then the kiss deepened as Hunter drank from Katherine's lips with the grace of a hummingbird gathering nectar at a scarlet hibiscus. The strong tongue plunged into the moist interior of her mouth, engaging hers in a sensual duel. Katherine whimpered softly as her lips closed, capturing his plundering tongue in a pantomime of the lovemaking to come.

"Now," he whispered huskily, dragging his heated lips down her throat, "tell me you don't want to make love to me."

Katherine looked up into the rugged face. The harshly hewn features seemed almost vulnerable in his desire. Her eyes were glazed and love-soft as they moved over his cheekbones, her fingers going up to trace the chiseled lines. Her other hand traced circular patterns on his black shirt.

"I can't," she whispered. "You know that, Hunter. I want to make love to you more than anything I've ever wanted in my whole life. But that doesn't make it right." Her dark eyes were melted chocolate, pleading with him to understand.

His hands moved down her body, molding her shape under the silk as if she were malleable clay. His eyes and his words mirrored the heated desire burning within his tense body as his fingers cupped her intimately, possessively, under the soft material.

"It doesn't make it wrong," he countered. "We're not hurting anyone, Kate."

Not at this moment, her whirling, spinning mind agreed. But what about tomorrow, when Hunter St. James disappeared from her life? Katherine had never been so buffeted by a set of circumstances. Ever since she'd first seen this man, he'd managed to shake her life to its very foundations. She felt like an exposed electrical wire, worn through until she was ready to spark and set fire to everything around them. If she allowed Hunter to make love to her, would she be strong enough to watch him walk away?

"I'm afraid," she whispered, her fingers tracing the hard line of his shoulders. "I can't even think straight when I'm near you, Hunter."

His mouth covered hers, as he moved swiftly to take advantage of her ambivalence. He kissed her with a possessiveness that swept away her last breath of opposition like a dry leaf under a stiff autumn wind. Her hands flung about the strong column of his neck as Katherine reached up to give him all that she was.

Chapter Six

Katherine's actions told him of her surrender more vividly than any words. Lightning coursed along her spine when she saw his eyes turn luminously tender as they glittered down at her.

"You'll see," the deep velvety voice promised, "we belong to each other, Kate. Nothing can ever change that."

The softly explosive whisper frightened her with its fevered intensity. She'd been right the first time she saw him in the post office, she realized with one last rational thought before she succumbed entirely to the mystical spell Hunter was weaving about them. Hunter St. James was imbued, to the bone, with a furious electric energy. She doubted if he ever did things halfway.

His hands skimmed the silk dress over her hips, followed in short order by her wispy underwear and panty hose. For a long, timeless moment his hungry eyes consumed her as they feasted on her warm, flushed body. Then his hands moved under her, gathering her up into his arms, pressing her to him, as if in sheer wonder.

It was a shock to Katherine's senses to feel her

naked flesh against this fully dressed man. It granted her a wild, wanton quality that was in itself vastly stimulating. Her fingers reached out to unfasten the buttons on his black shirt and her tongue sought to taste his warm, moist skin experimentally.

"Ah, Kate," he groaned softly at her teasing caress. As he pulled her more firmly into the cradle of his thighs, Hunter's need was revealed more vividly. He gasped as her tongue proceeded to sample each little bit of freed flesh down the rippling dark chest.

Katherine pulled her head back to look into his face, her eyes bright with interest at his reaction. "Do you like that?" she murmured, her tongue flicking across taut male nipples.

"I love it," he groaned as his hands tangled in her hair. "I swear, sweetheart, if I'd allowed that sheikh to take you home with him like he wanted, he'd have to get rid of the rest of the harem. None of them could hold a candle to you."

"That's nice," she whispered, her lips leaving the hard chest momentarily to brush against his own parted ones. "Hunter?"

"Hmmm?" His breath was warm and sweet in her mouth.

"Do you think he's really going to stay?"

"Let's talk about him later, okay, Kate? If you don't mind, I've got other things on my mind right now."

Katherine's full dark lips curved into a teasing, provocative smile. There was an element of power in this situation, she realized, and she enjoyed the knowledge that Hunter wanted her—needed her—so badly. She'd never been a tease, but right now, knowing the outcome as she did, the opportunity proved too tempting. Her sharp fingernail followed a line down the center of his muscled chest, leaving a raised red welt.

"Other things, hmmm?" she breathed seductively.

"Yes, you gorgeous little savage." Hunter's voice sounded like a bald tire running over a gravel road. His teeth came down in sharp, but careful retribution on her bottom lip, the slight pain an added jolt to her spinning senses.

Katherine's body was suddenly deprived of the warmth of his touch as Hunter rose from the bed, his golden, gleaming gaze locked with her own dark, wondrous one. She watched, entranced, as he divested himself of the rest of his clothing. Any of the carefully constructed aura of conservative sophistication that had survived the black suit joined the pile of clothing on the floor.

There was a predatory look to Hunter St. James. The vibrantly male body exuded a breathtaking primitive power and virility and the full extent of his desire for Katherine was boldly obvious as he stood before her, but he seemed to be waiting for some sign.

Of what? Approval? She wondered how any woman in her right mind could not approve unreservedly of Hunter in this situation.

"You're magnificent," she murmured honestly, treating the bronze, powerful physique to an openly admiring appraisal. "It should be against the law to cover all that with those three-piece suits."

"It'd get a bit chilly in Manhattan," he murmured. "Not to mention varied and assorted perils and thrills when riding the subway. But is that the artist talking? Or the woman?"

"Would it make a difference?" she asked curiously, not used to separating the two.

"Perhaps." His tawny eyes sparkled. "It would

depend on what each woman wanted to do with me. Now, if K. L. Michaels, the painter, simply wanted to stand me up on some pedestal while she painted pretty pictures, I think I might tend to feel used. On the other hand—"

"Hunter?" The low, throaty voice murmured his name, interrupting the lengthy answer.

Katherine watched as a dark brow quirked inquisitively. Then she held out her arms to him, welcoming him into her soft embrace.

"Hunter," she repeated his name, loving the sound of it on her lips, "come down off the damn pedestal to the woman."

Hunter made an inarticulate, low growl deep in his chest as he joined her on the bed. His hands caressed the curve of her spine to bring her into a close, intimate embrace, and his long legs tangled with her own on sheets emblazoned with rainbows.

There was a teasing riddle that kept her from losing her grip on reality.

"Hunter?"

Hunter placed both palms on either side of her head, levering himself up to gaze down at her, a look of gentle admonishment in his darkly amber eyes.

"Are you always this talkative? At this moment?"

"Of course not," she retorted, lifting her head from the softness of the pillow to pluck a light kiss against the softly smiling lips. "But I'm also not in the habit of tumbling into bed with virtual strangers. I'd like to know something." Her dark eyes softened to melted chocolate, pleading seductively.

Hunter sighed as he ran a smooth palm down the length of her body from shoulder to thigh, almost pushing the lingering query from her mind.

"Ask away," he said, on a thin thread of resignation.

"Why do you call me Kate?"

"Is that all?" He chuckled, lowering his cocoa-brown head to nuzzle the dark rosy crowns of her breasts. His eyes lit with satisfaction as they responded to his teasing lips. "You're my wild Kate, tempestuous and natural. And I'm going to tame you, my sweet shrew. Tame my own fiery savage."

Katherine opened her mouth to voice a loud complaint at his uncomplimentary terms, but her words were swallowed up by the swooping descent of his mouth, his warm sweet breath mingling with hers in an erotic perfume. The seductive movements of his lips plucked and pulled at the soft skin of her own, as if teasing them into a shape he preferred. His actions served to underline the message of those words with a crystal clarity.

Hunter St. James had every intention of taking charge and he was letting her know, none-too-subtly, that the time had come to cease this conversation.

His expert kisses created havoc in both her mind and her body, draining the strength from her. Hands, lips, and roving tongue moved over Katherine at will, branding her every pore with his burning touch as he sought to make her totally his. Hunter managed, in his quest, to discover erogenous zones Katherine hadn't dreamed existed, and as his lips feathered the back of her knee, reality receded far into the distance.

"Oh!" Katherine cried out a soft, surprised voice as those white teeth nipped at the delicate skin of her stomach. Her body arched toward him, yearning for his every touch.

"Hunter!" Her body seemed to have a mind of its own as it came alive under his clever hands. His short, square-cut nails running up the sensitive skin on the inside of her thighs created shafts of needlelike sensations. A dark force was invading her body, the heat surging through her veins like glowing, molten lava.

No one had ever touched her like Hunter St. James. No one had ever kissed her like this man. And Katherine had never succumbed so entirely to anyone as she did to the sensual mastery of his conquest.

Katherine's slim hands reached out to flutter across his shoulders like delicate, graceful birds, but Hunter was not to be coaxed from his design. His lips followed the heated path his hands had forged, fire following flammable vapor as he tasted of the warm satin of her skin.

It was when he reached and treated the warm heart of her to that tantalizing, aching intimacy that an all-consuming ache surged through Katherine. Her head tossed back and forth on the pillow, black threads of ebony silk becoming a wild tangle. Her back was arched in primitive, instinctive need, and she drank in short, shallow breaths. Katherine had always considered herself a woman who welcomed new experiences with open arms, delighting in the unusual, the exotic. But this—this dark hunger was threatening to consume her in hot waves and her body seemed to be as taut as a coiled spring, screaming for release.

"Hunter, I can't . . . I never . . . I don't know . . ." The words were broken and ragged, but they spoke volumes, and he stopped his erotic torture for a moment to brush the tangled strands of raven hair back from her face. His fingertips, which had been creating such sheer havoc, were gentle.

"I told you to trust me, Kate." His voice was a soothing, velvet caress. "You will. I promise. Don't worry about it, honey."

Katherine looked up into his eyes and allowed herself to be consumed, body and soul. Her hands encircled him as she brought his hard body down to cover her. Promises and trust were very nice words and ideas, but they weren't what she needed right now. Her nails dug into the firmly muscled buttocks as she moved her hips against him, encouraging him to fulfill her savage hunger.

"I was right." Hunter sucked in a harsh breath at the unexpected sharpness of her long nails. "You do need to be tamed, my wildcat. And fortunately, you've met your master."

"Master, are you?" Her sharp teeth nipped at the hard line of his shoulder, baiting the lion in his den.

"Master," Hunter muttered, pulling her hands from his back and holding them above her head out of harm's way. "And now, sweet, wild Kate, you're about to discover just how the master tames his shrew."

A breathless cry escaped her lips as he surged into her, taking ultimate possession. Katherine's hips rose from the mattress to welcome him, and for a long, timeless moment, both lovers seemed frozen, shattered by a force that shot like quicksilver through their bodies. Then Hunter began to move in a slow, deep rhythm, releasing Katherine's hands in order to put his fists under her, holding her to his hard male body.

She could feel him moving inside her as his lips drank long and thirstily from the sweet honey of her mouth. Once again Katherine was aware of that painful pleasure curling out from her middle region.

Her cries became muffled gasps of wonder as Hunter drove her deeper and deeper into the mattress, filling her with his aggressive, elemental male strength. Katherine moved to absorb the deep thrusts, her body dissolving into the mattress so she could no longer tell where she left off and the downy softness began.

"Hunter, what are you doing to me? Please . . . oh, God, Hunter!"

Her hoarse pleas for fulfillment were torn from her throat, desperate, tortured sounds. Then something shattered apart inside of her, like fine crystal disintegrating at a high note, and a blaze of rapture tore through her like a convulsion. Katherine was left shuddering with emotion as she clung helplessly to his shoulders, her long nails curving into his flesh like scarlet talons.

At her outcry, Hunter paused, hovering over her and allowing her to experience the fullness of her response to their passionate lovemaking. Then, seeming aroused by her uncensored reaction, he moved against her in a final display of power and glory, the triumphant shout seeming to claim her name seconds later as he joined her in a blazing, united flame.

Bathed in a warm, languid sensuousness, Katherine blinked slowly several times, attempting to get a grasp on every blissful sensation. She wanted to pinpoint every response, every exquisite emotion of this moment so she'd never forget it. As if she could, she mused, overcome with sheer pleasure.

She glanced down at the dark head resting on her glistening skin. Funny. Hunter was a large man. You'd think he'd be heavier than this. His weight was a warm comfort and she squirmed slightly, enjoying the feel of his body against hers.

"Umm. Am I too heavy?" The low voice rumbled against her throat.

"No," she answered, running her fingertips through the crisp, dark hair. "You're just right. Please don't move."

"Umph." Hunter's hand lazily traced down her leg. He seemed pleased with her decision.

Waves of warmth were still washing over her, rising and ebbing like a tide. Her head was finally clearing, but her body seemed more than willing to bathe forever in this golden afterglow of their lovemaking.

"Hunter?"

"Humph?" The glossy dark head burrowed deeper, like a forest animal seeking the warmth of his den for the winter months.

"Are you asleep?"

Hunter levered himself up, looking down at her, his eyes brimming with barely concealed amusement. "How could I possibly be asleep? You're the most talkative little thing I've ever met."

Katherine squirmed with irritation. "I'm not little."

He heaved a huge sigh, rolling off the warm haven of her body to lie beside her. Propping his head on his hand, his elbow sinking into her pillow, he made a long, leisurely study of her.

Katherine wished she hadn't brought it up. She knew that she wasn't fat, but her full curves were far more rounded than the ideal set by *Vogue*.

"No," he determined, his eyes warmly caressing her shapely five-foot-seven-inch figure. "Not little at all. Just right." He was practically setting a torch to her already warm, moist skin with those eyes.

"Hunter, I need to tell you something."

"What now?" Those full lips were barely able to hold back the hovering grin.

"This is serious, Hunter St. James!" Her brown eyes grew suddenly sober and sparkled suspiciously. Apparently they made their message clear, because the teasing glint vanished from the tawny amber gaze.

"I'm sorry. What do you have to tell me, Kate?"

She allowed her fingers to trace widening little circles on the soft pelt of cinnamon-dark hair covering his chest, unwilling to lift her eyes back to his waiting appraisal.

"I don't do things like this. Ordinarily." It was barely a whisper.

Long fingers with perfectly cut square nails reached out to cup her downcast chin, raising her troubled brown eyes to the face she'd been avoiding.

"Don't you think I knew that? Don't you realize I could tell by the way you responded in my arms?"

"And I suppose you're so damned experienced," she retorted sulkily.

Katherine felt like a prize fool for bringing the matter up. She was a grown woman, after all. She'd been married. Sex wasn't such a big deal these days. At least to most of the world. She was certain Hunter hadn't spent his life in some Tibetan monastery. Why should she feel the need to explain anything to him?

"I've shared a reasonable number of women's beds in my thirty-eight years," he answered, sending an inexplicable stab of jealousy through her with his bland admission. Katherine turned her head away.

"But," Hunter continued, reaching out to pull her head back to hold her startled dark eyes with the sheer strength of his will, "I've never shared with any woman what we've just had, Kate. That's all that's important."

Katherine felt herself drowning in the warm, inviting depths of his sincere eyes and she willingly succumbed, snuggling into his hard lean body. Pleased to be given a respite from the raised hackles they seemed to provoke within each other, they stayed that way for a long while. She could feel Hunter's soft, even breath on her hair and Katherine eventually glanced upward, to see if he'd fallen asleep.

But her eyes collided like brass cymbals with his dancing golden ones. "You're a feisty one, Kate. Stubborn as hell. It's no wonder no one's been able to corral you. But I believe I'm man enough to break you of those lovably irritating little traits."

"You think so, do you?" Her dark eyes flashed, preparing for another battle, when Hunter added to the insult by having the nerve to chuckle at her.

"I know so," he assured her in a rumbling deep voice. Pulling her to fit on top of him, his hands successfully reawakened those slumbering passions once again. "And, my darling, I think it's time for another lesson."

Chapter Seven

"Hunter?"

Katherine searched the large house, knowing in advance she wouldn't find him. Hunter had gone. Just as she'd wanted, he was out of her life.

He'd played out the charade last night, staying around to enjoy what she so willingly offered. Then he left. Sneaking out like a thief in the night. In fact, it was as if the man had never been here in the first place. Katherine had worked feverishly to complete the portrait of Spring Snow for the Manhattan show. Perhaps Hunter St. James had sprung from an overworked imagination.

Then she passed the mirror on her closet door and her fingers reached up to trace the outline of her full lips. No, that love-bruised mouth and those desperate, yearning dark eyes were evidence. She hadn't imagined a single thing.

Hunter St. James had stormed into her life two days ago, turning everything upside down before deserting her to face the rubble left in his wake. The truth, unpalatable as it might be, was that she'd responded with unadulterated abandon to a total stranger. A snowbird, sampling a bit of western scenery. He'd only sought her out in the first place to convince her to sell him *Spring Snow*.

Katherine thought about the price they'd agreed on while she'd been tutoring him yesterday afternoon, and she inwardly lashed herself for not raising the cost tenfold. At least then she'd have come out of this with something!

Katherine's shoulders had a tired, defeated slump to them as she went into the bathroom. She lifted her face to the shower, letting the water sting her skin like sharp needles as she rubbed the bar of soap viciously over her skin, in an attempt to scrub away every bit of her self-revulsion. And every bit of the taste and touch and scent of Hunter St. James from her body. She remained in the shower until the water turned icy cold, a formidable feat with her oversized water heater and solar reservoir. Her skin was red and raw, but she couldn't erase the feel of the man.

Throwing on her clothes, she looked at the bed with blatant distaste, eyeing its rumpled, love-tangled sheets. Bending down, she stripped the brilliant rainbow printed linens from the mattress, wondering if she should burn them. The intercom on the wall buzzed sharply, intruding on her black thoughts.

"Yes, Jack?"

"There's a truck here with a delivery. Should I send it up?"

That was a surprise. She'd known that the paintings she hadn't offered for sale from the gallery were being sent, but she wasn't expecting them until next week. Lord, she hadn't even called about *Spring Snow*. Hunter would hit the roof when he arrived back in Manhattan only to discover the painting had been returned to Carefree. To her.

A devil lurking somewhere deep within Katherine

urged her to keep the painting. Go back on her word as he'd done. Hadn't he promised he wouldn't hurt her? Hadn't he urged her to trust him? Well, she'd teach the man a thing or two about trust! The next time she made a deal with Hunter St. James, the terms would be written in triplicate, notarized, and stamped with a huge gold official seal. Actually, she corrected, the next time she made any kind of deal with him, there'd be a blizzard in hell.

"Thanks, Jack," she managed to answer the security guard. "Send it up."

Katherine stood before the huge crate, her arms still filled with the colorful sheets. Her dark-brown eyes had narrowed and she was observing it as if it might be full of poisonous snakes. Whatever the box contained, it certainly wasn't paintings. The size was all wrong.

"You've got the wrong house." She handed the clipboard with the pink form back to the delivery man. A pillowcase fluttered to the floor with the movement.

"You K. L. Michaels?" Bright-blue eyes observed her skeptically. Katherine realized that dressed in the cutoff jeans and the buttercup yellow T-shirt as she was, she probably appeared to be the maid.

"Yes, I'm K. L. Michaels, but—"

"Then this belongs to you. See? Right here on the top line." He turned the metal clipboard so she wouldn't have to read upside down. "K. L. Michaels. 15432 Desert Foothills Drive. Carefree, Arizona. This is yours, lady."

"I'm K. L. Michaels. And you've got the right address," she argued, "but the wrong crate. I'm suppose to be receiving a shipment of three good-sized paintings, not whatever this is." Her coffee-dark eyes narrowed even further. "What is this, anyway?"

Olive-drab shoulders lifted in a brief, uncaring shrug. "How should I know? Look, lady, just sign. See the invoice number? B7234. Same as the one stenciled on this crate. It's yours. Maybe someone's sent you a present. Just sign, okay? I've got a truckload of stuff I've gotta get delivered today."

Katherine shook her head in a negative gesture at the outstretched plastic pen. She didn't want to accept the wrong carton. If she claimed responsibility for this alien crate, how long it would take to return it and claim her own, proper delivery? They'd probably all drown in paper work attempting to undo the mixup.

"Great.! And just in time!"

Her startled gaze flew past the anxious delivery man to the impeccably dressed Hunter St. James.

"You expecting this, mister?" The man turned toward Hunter, relief stamped on every inch of his freckled face.

"Sure am. Where do I sign?"

"Right here." The clipboard swiveled rapidly in his direction, but Katherine could still see him take the pen and in a bold, dark script, sign K. L. Michaels.

"I'll show you where it goes," he instructed, moving past her in the open doorway.

"Hi, sweetheart. Miss me?" Hunter planted a quick peck on her open lips before leading the man with the orange hand truck down the long expanse of white-tiled hallway.

"Right in here," he said, moving into the den. Her den, she reminded herself firmly as she took up the rear of the little parade. Hunter's hand waved at a spot on the far wall and his dark, cocoa-colored head nodded approval as the crate was deposited. His hand slid into the slim navy pocket of his pants, withdrawing a folded bill which he pressed into the man's wide hand.

"Thanks a lot," Hunter said. "Sorry about the mixup. The little woman didn't know this was coming. Sort of a surprise, if you know what I mean." The amber eye winked, sparked with bright humor.

"Hey, mister, no problem. Anytime." His eyes brightened as he noted the denomination of the tip. "You have a nice day now. Enjoy your present, lady," he tossed back over his shoulder.

Hunter moved past Katherine, who was standing in the doorway to see the man out. When he returned, she was standing next to the huge crate, staring at it incredulously.

"Do you have a hammer, honey? One with a claw end?"

Katherine clutched the sheets to her bright T-shirt and eyed him suspiciously. "Hunter, what the hell *is* this?"

"It's a ticker-tape machine. At least that's what it'll be if we can get it out of the box. I had no idea they came like this. Where's your hammer?" he reminded her.

Katherine didn't know whether to laugh, cry or scream, so she managed to fit all three into the strangled sound.

"What am I suppose to do with a ticker-tape machine?"

He grinned at her in an incredibly boyish fashion, apparently finding nothing unusual in the fact that he'd just moved such an alien steel monster into her sunny, easel-filled room.

"Have a parade?" he asked blandly. "The way the

market's been jumping around lately, you should have loads of confetti."

"Hunter!"

He pulled ineffectively at one of the slats of lumber. "Honey"—he looked up from his squatting position, tawny eyes beguiling—"where's the hammer?"

"It's under the kitchen sink in the toolbox," she answered automatically, still feeling shell-shocked. "Hunter! Get back here!" She followed him out of the room, down the hall to the kitchen. "You are *not* going to uncrate that monstrosity in my den."

"If I don't uncrate it, Kate," he countered, bending down to move aside the boxes of dishwashing detergent and soap pads to reach the small, utilitarian toolbox, "I won't be able to use it."

"That's the point," she retorted, slamming the cupboard door, causing the stained birch wood to hit his head with a resounding crack.

"Hey!" Hunter rose slowly, rubbing his dark head as he eyed her grievously. "That hurt, Kate."

"There'll be a heck of a lot more of you hurting, Hunter St. James, if you don't get out of my house." She punctuated her warning with a swift kick against the cupboard door, and the neighboring one flew open.

Hunter's fingers moved against the small bump building on his scalp, as he eyed the pile of pots and pans that had spilled out around his feet.

"I could help you create a system for these things," he suggested helpfully, his face encouraging her to smile, "after we get the crate open."

"System? I've got a system, Hunter. I take the damn pots out of the dishwasher. I toss them into the cupboard, slam the door, and run like hell. Anything that stays in is exactly where it belongs. Exactly where I like it."

"I was just trying to help," he muttered.

"You want to help, Hunter? Get out of my house!" She threw the sheets at him, wishing they were made of something far more lethal than mere cotton percale.

Hunter ignored the sheets as they joined the pots and pans, and opened the cupboard door once again, rummaging through the cans of furniture polish and rolls of paper towels before extracting the small hammer.

"Whose house?" he asked casually.

"Mine!" Her voice was three octaves higher than normal.

"Mine, such as in K. L. Michaels?"

"Of course!"

He nodded and she felt a surge of sheer blinding fury at the self-satisfaction oozing from his every pore. He turned to leave, stepping over the pile of multihued sheets, and Katherine grabbed his arm to turn him back toward her.

"Where are you going now?"

Hunter waved the hammer, not threateningly, but just to remind her of its presence. "To uncrate my ticker-tape machine," he said with infuriating calm.

"You're going to do no such thing." Katherine grabbed for the hammer, feeling incredibly foolish as he held it easily out of reach above her head.

"Oh, no," he said. "You're much too wild to be handed a deadly weapon. Simmer down, Kate. I'm simply going to uncrate my machine and get to work. And if you don't mind, honey, I'd like a little quiet around here."

Katherine was struck dumb for a moment. She rubbed a weary hand across her eyes, hoping that this entire scene was nothing but a mirage that would be gone when she took her hand away. She peeked between her fingers warily. No such luck.

"Hunter, this is my house. And I intend to have you thrown out if you refuse to leave peacefully. You and your damn ticker-tape machine."

"I don't think you're in any position to do that," he returned calmly, unperturbed by her threat.

"This is *my house*, Hunter, and I want you out."

"This house belongs to K. L. Michaels, Kate, and I've got an entire roomful of witnesses who'll swear to their dying day that I'm that renowned painter of the old home on the range. And you, my dear, are my sweet and obedient fiancée, Katherine St. James. Now, if you don't mind, darling, I've really got to get to work."

Katherine thrust her hands behind her back, clutching her fingers together tightly as she worked to calm herself in the face of this overwhelming disaster. Her startled brown eyes widened to huge dark circles as she watched him.

"Hunter?"

He was pulling the slats off the wooden crate, but when he saw her face, he slowly put the hammer down on a white tile decorated with bachelor buttons and came over to her. His hands were hooked by the thumbs into his navy trouser pockets. There was no bright roguish teasing in his eyes as he surveyed her with gravity.

"Bad joke, huh?" The question was expelled on a slight, weary sigh.

Katherine nodded, her eyes sparkling with unshed tears.

"When you woke up this morning and found me

gone," Hunter surprised her by asking straightforwardly, "what did you think?"

She was uneasy under his silent survey and dropped her eyes to the tassels on his black loafers. She wondered irrelevantly about a man who traveled with such a wide assortment of dress shoes. So far, Hunter had worn a different pair to match each hand-tailored, superbly cut suit.

The man had a way of making her feel like Little Orphan Annie, for Pete's sake! And that crack about organizing her pots and pans ... she didn't doubt that he'd meant it. His kitchen probably had highly buffed, gleaming copper pans hanging from the ceiling on neat little hooks. And she'd bet her last nickel that they were all arranged in order by size. She and Hunter St. James didn't have a single, solitary thing in common. Well, perhaps one, she admitted honestly. But terrific sex wasn't something to base any type of long-lasting relationship on.

"Nothing, really," she answered finally, not lifting her eyes.

"If you're going to lie so often, you really should take a few lessons, Kate. You do it miserably."

The deep voice was laced with affection, hurting her instead of relaxing her as he'd meant to do. Katherine turned away, staring through eyes clouded with pain at the rolling green of the golf course.

"Hunter, I don't know what you think you're doing. I only know we had an agreement giving you the right to buy a painting. A painting that's still in New York. So why don't you go back there to pick it up and leave me in peace?"

She was struggling to maintain control over her life, and the warmth of him, as he came up behind her and looped those long fingers about her waist, wasn't helping. He drew her to him and she could feel the imprint of his male body against her back. His breath was a seductive warm breeze on her neck.

"There's so many reasons, Kate. For the moment, let's just focus on half a million essential little reasons why I'm going to be working out of here for the next week."

Katherine stiffened, fighting the enticing sensations the light embrace and the deep, vibrating voice were having on her.

"I suppose you mean Monica's money," she replied. "But she's already got that. We watched the sheikh present her with the check last night, remember?"

Hunter's palm moved down the long length of glossy black hair, stroking circles on her back where the waves finally ended. "I remember everything about last night." He pulled her hair back, brushing his lips onto the sensitive skin behind her ear.

"Hunter . . ." she pleaded on a soft whisper.

"He gave her a check," he reminded her, returning reluctantly to the subject at hand, "and checks can always be stopped. I'm not pretending to know a great deal about your friend's financial backer," he said with a bland tone that held a thin thread of irony. Katherine had the feeling that Hunter knew a great deal more than he was willing to admit. "But I do know his gifts are given spontaneously. And they've been known to have been taken back just as irrationally. Are you willing to take that chance?"

"We could tell him K. L. Michaels was called out of town," she hedged, chewing thoughtfully on a poppy-tipped fingernail. "Monica can keep him occupied watching rehearsals, and we'll stall."

"It won't work," Hunter stated flatly.

Katherine turned to him, tilting her chin stubbornly as she felt her strength returning.

"Why not?"

He gave her a lazy, winning grin. "Because, darling, in one hour, K. L. Michaels has a date to go riding with a certain Arab potentate. He's latched on to a friend who breeds Arabians in Scottsdale and we're driving out to the ranch."

Katherine's challenging look was replaced first by waves of sheer incredulity, then by an evil little grin. She eyed him with cynical appraisal. "Do you even know how to *sit* on a horse?"

Hunter laughed, a deep, self-assured sound that tugged at something deep within her. "It's got to be a helluva lot easier than sitting on the stuff you call furniture around this place." Long fingers reached out to ruffle her hair, before he returned to the task of uncrating his machine.

"Don't worry," he promised, his eyes dancing with merry devils as he looked back at her over his shoulder, "I won't do a thing to ruin K. L. Michael's illustrious reputation. On a horse or otherwise."

Katherine expelled an exasperated sigh, finding herself totally at a loss for words. He'd won this round, hands down. Surrendering for the moment, she walked slowly over to a sleek piece of curved teak and chrome, pulling out a hidden flush drawer.

"Hunter," she called out, tossing the item to him in a high, looping toss. "Just to keep you from breaking any more door panes."

He smiled his thanks, pocketing the set of keys before pulling another long nail out from the long slats of pine.

* * *

"I don't believe you!" Katherine stared up at the tall man lounging against her open door frame. She'd been lost in work, sketching as she sat cross-legged on her remade bed, sheets of white paper scattered all around her.

"Something wrong, ma'am?" he drawled laconically, tipping the black stetson back with the tips of his fingers.

Hunter was dressed in western clothes, vaguely similar to the ones she'd purchased. Yet the gaudy look of urban chic had vanished. For once, Hunter St. James looked as if he'd been born of the rugged southwestern desert rather than the crowded, bustling streets of New York City. Dark riding boots were lightly covered with dust, giving credence to the fact that he and Monica's sheikh had indeed been riding. The ornately tooled belt had been replaced by a dark-brown one with a simple, serviceable buckle. The only giveaway may have been the jeans. The color of the new pants was a bit too deep for a real cowboy's everyday attire. And they possessed a razor-sharp crease she couldn't remember seeing when he'd tried them on in the store.

When her gaze reluctantly returned to the bright-amber eyes gleaming under the black hat, he laughed. "I hope you realize this masquerade is making me feel like Dr. Jekyll and Mr. Hyde."

"You look like a native," Katherine complimented him truthfully. "Did you have a good time?"

His mouth quirked with good-natured humor. "Don't you really want to know how many times I fell off that damn horse?"

Her hand flew to her mouth in an attempt to stifle her laughter. "You didn't!"

Hunter shook his dark head. "Nope. Sorry to disappoint you, but I stayed on like the trooper I am. Must have some cavalry man's blood flowing through my veins." He rubbed his firm, denim-clad buttocks with a rueful expression. "Although I may never sit down again. I think I've been beaten black and blue."

Katherine threw him a pillow from the pile behind her. "Here, Hunter. Tie this on and you'll survive." She relaxed in the moment of shared humor.

His hands moved to the brass buckle. "Why don't you help?" he suggested. "That's kind of a tough spot for me to reach by myself."

"Hunter"—she squirmed uncomfortably—"If you're going to be staying here, let me show you the guest room."

He left the doorway toward the bed, moving some papers to sit beside her on the mattress. He lifted a thick swatch of jet-black hair and pushed it back over her shoulder as he gave her a long, level look. His fingers played lightly in the silken waves. "So that's the way it is?"

Katherine was drowning, not for the first time certainly, in those deep golden pools and she felt the paper wrinkle as her fingers closed tightly. The crackling sound seemed unnaturally loud in the long, discomforting silence.

"That's the way it has to be, Hunter," Katherine felt suspended as she awaited his objection.

His palm rubbed across the satiny royal-blue comforter, his expression one of reluctant resignation. "Is the bed in the guest room as comfortable as this one?"

"I think so," she murmured, feeling the heat rising in her cheeks at the memory of just how comfortable this queen-size bed had been the night before.

"The room wasn't furnished by the same madman

who ran amuck in the rest of the house?" His eyes teased unrepentently.

"I'll have you know that that's very expensive, imported hand-crafted furniture," she argued, pressing her lips together. "There are pieces out there copied from furniture displayed in modern galleries all over the world."

Her lips began to quiver and she turned her head away to stare out the window. But not in time. Long fingers cupped her chin, turning her gaze back to his own knowing one.

"You hate it too, don't you, Kate?"

"That's ridiculous," she protested with an obvious ring of deceit. "Would I have bought it if I hated it?"

"If that's the case," he argued, the muscle in his cheek betraying the grin that was threatening to break out and soften his rugged features, "then what are you doing, sitting in here like the lone little Indian on this bed while you work?"

"That's none of your business. Oh, damn you, Hunter," Katherine broke into bubbling laughter. "You're right. It's uncomfortable. You have to be a contortionist to sit on it. Monica's decorator assured me I'd love it if I just lived with it for a while, but I don't. It's being replaced as soon as possible." She crossed her arms across her chest. "The colors and the tiles, however," she stressed firmly, "are my choices."

"And they're lovely, sweetheart," he said, bringing her face toward him for a light, heart-tugging kiss.

"Hunter—" Katherine pulled away, rubbing her palms on her bare legs. It wasn't that she didn't want to kiss him. Good Lord, it had rapidly become her favorite pastime. It was what that one kiss would inevitably lead to. Katherine knew with a crystal-clear certainty that she never wanted to reexperience the feelings she'd had when she'd found him gone this morning.

The trick was to keep herself from getting involved with Hunter St. James, and her mistake had been in attempting to avoid entanglement with the man before first mastering the easy stuff—like pulling an elephant out of a hat or piloting the space shuttle.

His voice was sincerely apologetic, as were the amber eyes studying her thoughtfully. "I forgot," he confessed. "It's damn hard to keep my hands off you, Kate, but I'll do my best." He treated her to a soft, coaxing smile. "Have you noticed that when you're not backing away—or spitting like a riled cat in a thunderstorm—that we get along just fine?"

"Maybe," she responded with far more poise than she felt. "I'll have to give it some thought."

"You do that," he suggested, rising to stand next to the wide, comfortable bed. "Oh, by the way, did I get any more deliveries today?"

She looked up at him curiously. "No. Were you expecting something else? A truckload of overstuffed furniture, perhaps?"

"Just a computer," he replied, leaving the room with a lithe, easy stride. "But I can work for a while longer without it, I suppose."

Katherine stared at the broad back. A ticker-tape machine. A computer. What made her think she could keep Hunter from seizing her heart when she couldn't stop him from taking over her house?

When she looked into the den later, searching for Hunter, he was gone and a note addressed to her was on the desk. He'd be eating at Monica's. They were giving the sheikh his first taste of barbecued steak. Katherine was advised not to wait up. They'd probably go out afterward and try out whatever nightlife the town had to offer.

Katherine crushed the note between her palms, flinging it into a chrome wastepaper basket. Then she went into the kitchen and put a frozen chicken pie into the oven, suddenly hating the idea of eating alone.

Chapter Eight

Katherine moaned softly, her erotic dream interrupted by an insistent clattering that was doing its best to wake her up. Rolling over onto her stomach, she pulled the pillow over her head in an attempt to block out the noise. She squeezed her eyes tight, conjuring up Hunter's image.

"No, no, no!" she said out loud, using all her powers of concentration to focus on the sensuous dream and not the sound of cabinets being opened down the long hallway. One eye peeked open just a slit, taking in the deep indigo-blue shadows in her bedroom. It was still the dead of night. She was imagining things.

She gripped the corners of the soft, down pillow more firmly, burrowing into the mattress with renewed determination. She refused to wake up. The ruckus escalated, the clamorous sound of metal crashing against metal bringing her fully awake. Her eyes slid to the whirling anniversary clock and she shook her head, wondering what could have gotten into Hunter now. Katherine knew exactly what time he'd gotten in because she'd lain awake, staring at the shadows on the ceiling, until she'd heard his car pull into the garage. Not even Hunter St. James could consider two hours a sufficient night's rest.

"What are you *doing*?" She belted the emerald silk robe, eyeing him with unfeigned irritation.

"I was looking for the coffee," he answered amicably. "Did I wake you up?"

"Wake me up?" Katherine's voice hit an unnaturally high register. "*Wake me up?* What in the world gave you a foolish idea like that? Why should I be asleep at this hour of the morning? Why should *anyone* be asleep?" Her hands thrust into the deep pockets of her robe, curling into tight fists.

"I woke you up," Hunter decided, eyeing her cautiously. "I tried to be quiet, honey. Would you like some coffee?"

"Hunter, if it isn't too much trouble, could you tell me just why you felt moved to make coffee in the middle of the night?"

"I've got work to do. I always drink coffee when I work." He shrugged. "It's a habit I've developed."

Her dark brow shot upward. "I've developed a few little idiosyncrasies of my own, Hunter, and one of them is sleeping. What work could you possibly have to do at this hour? Have you taken to moonlighting as a vampire?"

He shook his dark cocoa-colored head. "Do you know that you look gorgeous? Even at this time in the morning? Incredible." His eyes swept over her with absolute approval.

Katherine's hands left the pockets long enough to tug at the green satin belt, drawing it tighter. "Then you *do* know what time it is?"

"Of course," he responded with maddening nonchalance. "That's why I'm up. To check the market opening."

Crazy. He was certifiably crazy.

"Hunter, it's not nearly time for the stock market to open yet. In fact, even hypertensive New Yorkers are all tucked away in their little trundle beds, awaiting the delightful music of banging garbage cans to rouse them from their innocent slumbers."

"London," he answered unexpectedly.

Katherine pushed back her tumbled hair, combing it ineffectively with her fingers. "What?"

"I'm checking the market opening in London." It was stated with such a normal, matter-of-fact tone that she realized he wasn't kidding. This man actually crept out of a warm bed in the middle of the night in order to call London.

"That's a long-distance call," she complained.

"Last time I checked."

"You could've asked."

"I have a credit card, Kate. You won't be billed."

Katherine knew she sounded picky and churlish. But then, she thought, this was a ridiculous conversation to be having at any hour.

"Oh. Why don't you call Zurich while you're at it?" she suggested with saccharine sweetness.

"I did."

Oil and water. That's what she and Hunter were. Shake vigorously and they'd come together for a brief interlude, but left on their own, they'd be bound to separate. Katherine had never known anyone to creep about in the dark of the night, checking on the stock market. In fact, she could count on the fingers of one hand the number of her friends who even bothered to read the financial pages of the newspaper with any degree of regularity.

Now, here she was, standing in her kitchen at four o'clock in the morning, while a near-naked stockbroker checked his holdings in Europe. Which of them was more insane? Hunter, for doing it? Or she, for actually standing here watching?

"Are you going back to bed?"

A slow, lazy smile creased his rugged features. "Is that an invitation?"

Katherine thrust nervous fingers once more through her sleep-tousled hair, only ruffling it further. "That's not it at all. I was just wondering if this was your usual hour to wake up. I mean, are you up for good now?"

Wrong. Even at this hour she realized that had been a stupid thing to say. A dark-crimson flush burned her cheeks as the golden eyes sparked with a sudden lazy heat. Hunter rubbed his jaw thoughtfully, relishing the effect the long, significant silence was having on her. He was wearing only his jockey shorts, and she didn't dare allow her gaze to move away from his face.

"Funny you should mention that," he drawled on a low, seductively pitched note. "Why don't I just call London a little later?"

Katherine felt as if she'd been nailed to the floor, unable to move as the lithe, muscular body moved toward her. His hands spanned her slender waist, drawing her lightly into the uncompromising maleness of his rock-hard body as his lips signaled a halt to all financial business. They moved with infinite tenderness across the uplifted planes of her face and she felt a slight shock of desire as the rough, sandpapery morning beard grazed her skin.

"Not this time, Hunter," she said, twisting free. She backed away from him, keeping her eyes glued to a spot behind his left shoulder. There wasn't a spot on

Hunter St. James that was even marginally safe for her to look at.

She was stopped as her back came against the butcher-block counter, and Hunter placed his hands on either side of her, effectively blocking escape. One hand left the oiled wood long enough to reach out and loop a long strand of ebony hair behind her ear.

"You weren't complaining the other night," he murmured. His eyes were glowing amber beacons, like traffic warning lights. Proceed with caution. A message it was high time she heeded.

As he leaned toward her, Katherine couldn't deny that the powerful male physique was startlingly beautiful in its near nudity. Hunter appeared to have absolutely no qualms about appearing this way, but oddly enough this served to bolster her teetering resolve. No doubt he was quite used to willing women admiring the expertise of that splendid body. The way he used it to his advantage, even now, bespoke of worlds more experience than she could lay claim to. She refused to make it all that easy for him, even if her determination was a little late in coming.

"Hunter," she faltered for a moment at the dark look of passion so very near her, "I'm going back to bed. You go make your calls."

He moved backward, dropping his hands to his sides. She was free to go now, but something held her a moment longer. Wide brown eyes searched his face, looking for some sign of that earlier rising passion. Or irritation. Or even anger. But he'd slid a mask down over his features, and his expression was unreadable.

"Sure," he replied uncaringly. "Sweet dreams." He turned away, and as she escaped the room, she heard the buttons of her Trimline telephone being punched with far more force than was necessary. Katherine collapsed into her bed and fell into a restless sleep.

Following the enticing aromas drifting through the house, Katherine found Hunter busy at the kitchen stove. One hand was lifting a cup of coffee to his lips while the other was deftly twirling a small frying pan with maddening expertise. She wondered why it should bother her that the man seemed able to do everything so damn perfectly.

"Good morning," he greeted her with a dazzling grin. "Care for some breakfast? I'll split this omelet with you."

"No, thanks. Coffee's fine." Katherine glared at him, finding it difficult to work up any anger when faced with his cheery good mood. "I see you've made yourself right at home."

He flipped the mushroom omelet onto a plate. It looked like a picture from a cookbook, she noticed with a rush of annoyance.

"I'm sorry," he said, handing her a cup of coffee, "did you want to cook my breakfast?"

"Me? Of course I didn't! Remember, Hunter, you're not a guest in this house. You're nothing but a squatter. Uninvited and unwelcome."

"Are you always this cranky in the morning?" His fork stopped halfway to his mouth and he eyed her warily, as if he expected her to dump the coffee in his lap at any moment. "Yesterday you slammed a cupboard door on my head and tried to crown me with a hammer. Today you're begrudging me two little eggs. I can tell I'm going to have to learn to stay out of your way until you've had your coffee. Which, by the way, I'm more than willing to serve you in bed from now on."

He leaned over and placed a hard kiss on her lips, effectively staying the protest that had been forthcoming. "You are, however, still gorgeous. Even when you're thinking about throwing coffee at me."

How did he know? She slowly removed her hands to her lap. "I wasn't thinking any such thing."

"Sure," he mumbled, taking a bite of toast. "By the way, what are your plans for today?"

Katherine shrugged. "I don't know. I suppose I'll work on the sketches I brought back from Window Rock. I don't map out my day's activities with all the precision of the Joint Chiefs of Staff preparing for armed invasion, Hunter. That's your way. I pretty much take things as they come."

"Great. Then you can come riding with us."

"Us?"

"Us. K. L. Michaels, reclusive western artist; Ahmed, sheikh of the burning sands; and Monica."

"Monica? On a horse?" Her dark winged brows lifted and her lips curved into a full smile. "Watching you and Monica attempting to stay astride a pair of horses is bound to be an experience," she decided. "I'll go."

Hunter grimaced slightly. "I'm not sure that it's a positive sign in the state of our relationship when the only reason you want to spend the day with me is to watch me fall onto my rump," he muttered. "But I suppose a guy's got to start somewhere."

Katherine was well used to Monica's theatrical approaches to life, but even she hadn't expected the fawn breeches, green velvet blazer, highly polished black boots, and the jaunty little cap with a red feather in it. The woman looked ravishing, even if she did appear to be an extra from *National Velvet*. Katherine rubbed her palms on her jean-clad thighs, knowing that she was quite properly dressed for an afternoon at a ranch. Still, she couldn't help feeling like a tattered waif they'd dragged in off the desert.

It was scant consolation that Monica rode horrendously, bouncing up and down on the sleek Arabian mare. The men appeared to have little interest in her riding ability. After half an hour, Katherine could stand no more of it and turned her horse abruptly, following a steep trail up the hillside. She didn't turn when she heard the plodding of steady hoofbeats behind her. She knew who it was.

"Taking a shortcut?"

She didn't answer, but applied a slight pressure with her knee to move her horse to the left, blocking Hunter's passage as he attempted to come up beside her.

"Monica must really be desperate for that money," he offered, still attempting to strike up a conversation. "She's going to be stiff as a board tonight. Not to mention black and blue."

"You should know," Katherine snapped, "since you've spent the last thirty minutes watching that particular bit of Monica's anatomy bounce up and down."

She still hadn't allowed him to pass, so Katherine missed the look of pleasant surprise that passed across his face.

"I thought I'd made myself clear on that subject. I prefer my women with a bit more flesh. Something to warm a man on a cold night," he teased.

"In the first place, I'm not your woman. And we don't have that many cold nights here, Hunter."

"We do in Manhattan," he argued. "When I get chilled this winter, can I invite you to come warm my bed?"

She turned abruptly in the saddle, her face bright

with anger. "That's all you think about, isn't it? Getting me into your bed."

"No."

"You could've fooled me."

"I also think about getting you into a deep warm bathtub. And onto a tropical sun-warmed beach, and bundled under a thick pile of furry blankets, being driven through Central Park in a horse-drawn sleigh. Have you ever made love in a sleigh, Kate?"

"Of course not."

"Good. It'll be a first for both of us then."

He'd effectively sidestepped her continual blockage of the path, maneuvering the priceless Arabian dangerously near the edge of the steep winding trail. He reached over, taking the reins from her, and stopped her horse.

"Why do you keep fighting it?" Hunter's lion eyes were grave as they held her wary gaze. "You didn't come out here to watch Monica make a spectacle of herself on that horse, and you haven't spared two glances toward the sheikh. Which, by the way, has broken his heart, I think. He's quite entranced with you, you know."

"Sure," Katherine muttered, mentally comparing herself to the brilliant flame of a woman somewhere back down the trail. "Why in the world would he be at all interested in the gray moth when he's got the butterfly in the palm of his hand?"

"It's your naturalness," he replied simply. "It's appealing and damn exciting, actually. Makes a man suspect you'd be just as uninhibited in bed, Kate."

Katherine felt the dark flush rising on her skin from the memory of just how true that had been. With Hunter. Only with him.

"Hunter," she murmured, shaking her head in a

gesture of regret. She couldn't deny that she found him attractive. She would never be able to deny that she wanted him. But Hunter St. James was like quicksand—one false step and she'd be in over her head.

"Kate," he answered, leaning across the small space between then, reaching out to cup her chin in his hand. His thumb played along the edge of her mouth.

"I want you so very much, Kate. Do you know how hard it is to try to sleep on the other side of the house from you when I've experienced your warm welcome?"

Katherine knew she should look away, knew she should run from the sensual message stirring in Hunter's golden eyes. But she didn't.

"I know," she whispered.

"Oh, Kate . . ." Hunter slid to the ground, taking both pairs of reins and flipping them lightly around a tree limb. Then he put his hands about her waist and lifted her easily from the horse, holding her unnecessarily close as he lowered her down along his strong body.

His hands remained on her waist, his fingers digging into her flesh as his desirous gaze warmed her face. "You're already sharing your name and your house with me, sweet Kate," he murmured as his fingers ran up and down her side, creating little shafts of need that were just this side of pain. "Will you share one thing more?"

"What one thing, Hunter?"

"A kiss? I've been wanting to kiss you since I got home last night. I wanted to kiss you when you tied into me about waking you up. And I wanted to throw that damn omelet down the garbage disposal and taste your sweet lips instead for my breakfast. I don't want to wait any longer, but I need you to want to kiss me too, Kate."

"Oh, Hunter." She sighed, flinging her arms about his strong neck. "Heaven help me, but I want that too."

His lips lowered, covering her own with an intensity that spoke of his barely restrained hunger. His mouth moved against hers as if he were indeed starving to death and her lips were a moist, fresh fruit. His tongue circled the full dark lips, stroking, tasting, teasing the flesh before sliding inside to run along the hard line of her teeth.

Katherine's hands caressed his sun-warmed back as her head fell back willingly under his tender assault. Her teeth parted, just slightly, inviting the strong tongue inside, where it searched out all the hidden corners of her dark, moist mouth.

Hunter's hands moved below her waist, grasping at the firmly curved bottom and kneaded her flesh through the denim, his fingers causing eddies of warmth to skim down her thighs. As if knowing the effect his hands had on her, Hunter moved them lower, holding tightly to the back of her legs to bring her nearer.

Kate could hear the soft, feminine sounds escaping her lips and filling the air around them. She knew that once again Hunter St. James was imprisoning her in his sensual lair. She tugged at his cotton shirt, opening the snaps to allow her palms to move in hard circles against his chest, the crisp hair teasing the sensitive skin of her palms, heightening every sensation.

In response, Hunter's fingers opened the buttons on her yellow plaid western shirt, allowing his warm, agile fingers to trace a trail down along her bared throat, under and around each breast. Katherine's nipples responded under the lacy bra she wore, but Hunter seemed willing to continue his leisurely caresses, bypassing the taut dark berries that seemed to be reaching for his touch. When her need to feel those hands against her overcame her atypical shyness, Katherine reached down and took his hands, lifting them to cover her breasts, issuing a sigh of relief as his fingers alternately tugged and massaged at her yielding flesh.

"So, so nice, Kate," he murmured, his head lowering as he pushed down the scalloped lace border, lifting one breast from its confinement to taste of it with his warm sensuous lips.

Katherine's fingers laced through the crisp, dark hair, her body threatening to burst into flame at any moment. Just as she was prepared to agree to anything Hunter might suggest to ease this spiraling desire, they were both almost knocked off balance by a collision with the hindquarter of Hunter's Arabian mare, who sidestepped into them.

"I think she's jealous." Katherine laughed on a weak gasp as Hunter caught her, saving her from tumbling onto the hard, rocky ground. "You've just too many females in your life, Hunter St. James. You shouldn't try to spread yourself so thin."

He made an inarticulate grunt deep in his throat as he pulled the lace back up over her firm breast and rebuttoned her shirt. His own, she noted, he left undone to the waist.

"I only want one," he muttered. "But I suppose it's just as well. A few more minutes and we both would've had to spend the evening picking cactus needles out of each other's skin."

"Think so, do you?" she asked, pulling herself back up onto her snowy-white Arabian.

"I know so, Kate. So do you."

A very comfortable silence surrounded them for a time as they rode the horses, side by side, along the trail. Every once in a while, as the path narrowed, Hunter would turn his mare inward, brushing his leg against hers, and Katherine would feel a nice comfortable warmth. He had been right about one thing: whenever she could relax around the man, she actually found herself enjoying the moment.

"You ride quite well, actually," she said.

"It's not that difficult. I can fake it well enough as long as nobody takes me out for a fast canter. Not that I've succeeded in discovering what fascination it is these stupid animals seem to hold for humans."

As if protesting his derogatory words, Hunter's mare whinnied loudly.

"Now you've done it, Hunter." Katherine laughed. "You've hurt her feelings. She'll probably end up throwing you."

"She wouldn't dare. I've already got myself one female who's too dangerous to turn my back on. I sure as hell don't need another."

"Correction." she stated firmly. "You don't have me, Hunter. I thought we'd made that perfectly clear."

"If you really think that," he answered, "then you're as dumb as this horse, Kate, and I doubt if that's possible."

"Do you talk this way around the shiekh? I don't imagine he'd be thrilled to discover that K. L. Michaels hates horses. Especially Arabians."

"No. I'm on my best behavior with him. I told you, honey, I wouldn't do anything to hurt you. The man thinks I adore these big-teethed, four-footed monsters."

She returned the smile, shaking her head in light frustration. "Oh, damn," she muttered.

"What's the matter?"

Hunter watched, perplexed as Katherine slid off her horse and bent down, lifting the right hind leg. "A stone," she said, gouging at the stubborn pebble. She shook her head in frustration. "It's wedged too tightly. Looks as if I walk back."

Hunter was beside her in one quick motion, lifting her up onto his western saddle before swinging easily up behind her.

Katherine experienced a strange mixture of dread and pleasure as he clicked quietly to his mare, turning the horse with a light flick of the reins. His warm bare chest was firm against her back, the hard pillar of his thighs pressing into the back of her legs. As the horse walked slowly back to the ranch, Katherine's horse following docilely, the soft, swaying motion caused their bodies to rub together in a nice way.

"I take it back," Hunter murmured, his breath warm on the back of her neck as he lifted her heavy hair to kiss her warm nape.

"Take what back?" she asked softly, feeling her warming flesh practically melting into his.

"That nonsense about me hating horses. I'm coming to the conclusion that the animals are man's best friends."

Katherine entered the den to find Hunter bent over lettuce-green sheets of computer printouts. They'd been in the house together for five days now and she doubted if she'd seen him for a total of thirty minutes. If he wasn't out running around with Monica and her sheikh, playing K. L. Michaels, he was locked up in here with his mechanical toys. The ticker-tape machine seemed to run continually, and the first day she'd sworn several times to take the hammer to it. Now, she realized, glancing at it, she never really heard it unless she thought about it.

"Dr. Jekyll, I presume."

Hunter looked up, his eyes lighting with approval, the deep grooves on either side of his mouth growing even deeper with the smile. She was wearing a natural gauze dress, reminiscent of a Mexican wedding dress. The gathered neckline was off the shoulder and the sleeves were full and trimmed in lace. The tiered skirt came down to her ankles. The look was delicate, a change from her usual vibrant hues, and unabashedly romantic.

"It depends," he answered slowly, his tawny gaze growing to a deep topaz. "If you dressed up that way for Mr. Hyde, I'll be happy to go put that cowboy suit on. Even if it does smell like a horse." Hunter scratched his head thoughtfully. "Which one of those guys got the girl?"

"I think Dr. Jekyll got the nice ones, and Mr. Hyde the wild ones."

"I don't suppose I could be so lucky as to have my cake and eat it too?"

A dark eyebrow arched, encouraging him to elaborate.

Hunter leaned back precariously in the contoured suede chair, placing his elbows on the curved chrome arms. Linking his fingers together, he rested his chin on them, eyeing her with a glint of pleasurable lust.

"I mean, to know a real lady who possesses the soul of a wild woman?"

"That's asking quite a lot, Hunter."

"I know. But I've discovered I'm a selfish man, Kate."

She perched on the corner of the desk. "Selfish?"

"Selfish," he reaffirmed, leaning forward to run his hand along her arm. "A week ago, all I wanted in life was to take *Spring Snow* home from the Waring Gallery. I did everything but break and enter to get it. That was my mission."

She decided to ignore the fact that breaking and entering was, indeed, how he'd gotten into her house in the first place. "A mission you've accomplished Hunter. She's yours."

"She is. But then I met you and I had to hold you in my arms. I had to get you to admit you felt that same shock of recognition and need I'd suffered. I wanted to make love to you, Kate."

"And you've accomplished that, too. Are you always so successful in your missions?"

"Always," he answered without any degree of false modesty. "But that's because I never go after anything I'm not totally committed to. That way I never back down. Most people do."

"So," Katherine said with brittle lightness, "you simply outwait them. Like a spider in a web."

"Sometimes. Other times a more active tactic works better."

She absently picked up a silver letter opener and toyed with it, considering his words. "If you're after what I think you're after, Hunter, don't you think you should be keeping your battlefield strategies to yourself?"

Hunter reached out and took the metal object from her hand. "Sorry, sweetheart. I never talk about potentially dangerous subjects when you've got those lovely hands on a potential weapon. I had trouble pulling my hat down over that bump on my head."

An embarrassed flush warmed her cheeks.

"Now," he continued, putting the opener on a shelf behind him, "what do you think I'm after?"

Katherine met his gaze straight on. "Me."

"Good guess. But you've had lots of hints. What else?"

"There's more?" The self-assured expression faded.

"As you've pointed out, darling, I've already made love to you. Don't you want to know exactly why I'm hanging around this dusty burg?"

Katherine slid off the teak desk, her temper flaring. "This is not a dusty burg. It's a delightful, quiet community inhabited by individuals who don't feel the need to keep themselves artificially stimulated by constant, frenetic activity."

Hunter unfolded gingerly from the chair to stand over her, his fingers resting lightly on her bared shoulders.

"I think you mean that," he murmured, as if surprised.

She glared up into his suddenly serious face. "Of course I mean it, Hunter! I love Arizona. And Carefree symbolizes everything I've found that pleases me about the state. The people, the weather, the lifestyle. The freedom to do what I want when I want, without artificial deadlines. It's *you* I can't understand. I'm beginning to think you're serious about liking New York."

"Of course I do! The theaters, the energy, the adrenaline of trading on the floor when you're ankle-deep in paper and you can hardly hear yourself think, the restaurants—"

"The blackouts, the transit strikes, the air pollution," she added dryly, her face set in a firm, argumentative mask.

Hunter expelled an enormous sigh. "We're not going to get anywhere trading pros and cons," he said. "Why don't we discuss the advantages of each place unemotionally?"

"All right," Katherine agreed. "But let's go out in the garden where it's peaceful."

"It's not exactly pandemonium in here, darling," he said, gazing about the hushed interior of the large room.

"That's true, Hunter. But it's almost time for the sunset. Something you don't have in New York."

He gathered up the sheets of paper and stacked them neatly in the far left-hand corner of the desk. All the edges, she noted with a ridiculous rush of irritation, were lined up to a honed uniformity.

"Of course we have sunsets," he argued, adjusting one final sheet with the precision of a NATO general preparing for rifle inspection. "And they're three hours earlier. You just get a rerun."

She slipped her hand in his, leading him to the garden courtyard. "You have sunsets you can seldom see, due to the gray, smoky cloud hovering over the city. And out here, Hunter, the sun sets all the way into the ground. Not smack into the sixty-seventh floor of some high-rise office building."

"Do you believe in reincarnation, past lives, any of that?" Hunter asked suddenly.

Katherine had been engrossed in studying him, so alien in her sleepy, sun-filled garden. The oxford-cloth white shirt, she supposed, with its button-down collar was less formal than the white-on-white silk she'd been seeing. The slim, striped tie, however, negated any improvement with the shirt. As he leaned back in the chair, he put his feet up on a wrought-iron table and thrust his hands deeply into the pockets of his gray slacks. The loafers today, she noted with an artist's eye for detail, were suede, again more casual than the soft calfskin. But she'd bet her eyeteeth they were Gucci. Hunter was chic, elegant, and what was even more upsetting, entirely wrong. Wrong for this relaxed western setting. And wrong for her.

The question about reincarnation was posed with a studied nonchalance, and Katherine had an eerie feeling the man was leading her directly into trouble.

"No," she answered, returning her gaze to his questioning eyes. "With my imagination, I've been able to create things that sometimes seem like memories, but they're not."

A pink glow was tinting the puffy clouds overhead as the last vestige of the setting sun gilded the land. In a last, brilliant, gaudy show, the molten ball of fire splintered the sky with intense colors as it flung itself into the desert floor. The soft mauve haze hung over them long after the sun had set, bathing them in a half-lit world.

"That painting, *Spring Snow*—how were you able to reach out and capture her so well?" His question came at her from out of the blue.

Katherine lifted her head a fraction of an inch, like a wary deer scenting the presence of man in the forest. Hunter was on the prowl again, the seemingly casual question obviously a predatory ploy.

"You only saw the finished product," she stated tentatively. "That painting took five years of false starts."

"I suppose it's no coincidence that you look like her." His amber eyes held a thoughtful appraisal.

"She was my great-grandmother," Katherine admitted, deciding that it certainly wouldn't hurt to tell him. Surely what they'd shared in her brass bed was far more intimate than the knowledge, and perhaps he'd understand why she'd been so reluctant to sell it.

His attitude didn't reveal if he'd been surprised by the revelation. "*Spring Snow*," he murmured, "how did you come to name it that?"

"It was her name. In the spring, the cottonwood trees fill the air with their soft, fluffy white blossoms. The Indians who live along Havasu Creek call it the spring snow. She was born during that time." Katherine shrugged gracefully. "Thus the name."

"I like it," he approved. "Five years," he mused, as if to himself. Then, again to her, "Why were you so intrigued?"

Katherine felt as if she were treading a very narrow path here. There was an emotion lying buried just under the surface of this conversation that she couldn't put her finger on. She knew him well enough to know that Hunter didn't engage in casual conversation. There was a reason behind this line of questioning, but what was it? If she attempted to shrug it off, he'd just keep digging. She knew that. He'd chip away and chip away until he'd broken down her protective barrier.

"I'd spent a lifetime listening to stories about her," she said, the nerves tightening in the pit of her stomach. "She'd had an unusual life."

"Not altogether a happy one, I'd suspect."

Her dark eyes at first flew open at the casually issued statement, then narrowed as she searched the harsh planes of his face. "Why do you say that?"

He shrugged his wide shoulders. "It was in her eyes, an underlying sadness. It looked as if she'd lived with it a long time and had become resigned to carrying it with her the rest of her life."

Katherine wondered whether she'd actually captured her great-grandmother that well, or if Hunter had an uncanny eye for detecting the faintest nuances in art. Whatever, he'd left the quiet statement hanging in the soft, perfumed air between them and waited for her to pick up on it.

"I suppose," she began with a sigh, "that it wasn't a very unusual story, for the times. She was still young when she married a French trapper and left her village to live with him at the fort. When the fur trade dropped off, he left her to return to St. Louis."

"Is that the reason for the sorrow behind her beautiful face?"

Katherine shook her head, wondering as she did so why she couldn't just agree and drop the subject. "No. You see, she fell in love with a young cavalry officer at the fort. It was a love that was destined to fail for a lot of reasons. The outcome was that he went back east and Spring Snow stayed in Arizona." Katherine grimaced slightly. How hard it must have been to see their love torn asunder by the times and by circumstances beyond the two lovers' control.

He digested the remark silently, then he smiled, as if at a private joke.

"Hunter?" Katherine invited comment.

He regarded her across the intervening space, attractive lines fanning out from the corners of his eyes.

"I'm sorry," he apologized for his lapse, "I was just thinking."

Katherine sensed some emotional sleight of hand and her fingers curled together in her lap. "About what?"

"Us. Isn't it nice that there's nothing to keep you from allowing yourself to fall in love with me? I'd hate to see that sadness in your gorgeous, velvety eyes.

So"—the smile widened coaxingly—"why don't you just give in, Kate? It's inevitable, you know."

Katherine's temper flared as she scrambled to her feet. "You"—she jabbed a crimson-tipped finger at the grinning man sitting across from her—"are arrogant, despicable, infuriating—" She paused for breath and a new list of adjectives.

"And right," Hunter filled in for her. "Don't forget that."

"And stupid!" Her temper was completely lacerated as she viewed the unruffled Hunter St. James. His easy grin extended all the way to those dancing amber eyes and she looked around wildly for something, anything, to hurl at his dark head.

"I knew I was right to take that letter opener away. Taming you is turning out to be harder than I'd ever imagined. Why don't you give up the idea of that right cross you're about to flatten me with and let me take you out to dinner?"

"What?" Katherine stared down at him, then followed his gaze down to her right hand, which was curled into a threatening fist. "Oh." Her fingers uncurled slowly as she rubbed her palm against her gauze skirt. A half-smile hovered apologetically on her lips. "Do you do that on purpose?"

Dark brows lifted on the wide brow as one hand flew dramatically to his chest. "Do what?" he inquired with an exaggerated innocence.

"Make me angry just to liven things up around here."

"Aha! Then you agree that they could use some livening up." The glimmer of amusement lurking in Hunter's eyes almost set her off again, but Katherine took several deep breaths, achieving control.

"No," she said, "I just think you need a little stimulation. Your body probably goes into cardiac shock if it isn't operating at warp speed."

"You're all the stimulation I need, Kate." Rising to take her hand in his, Hunter rubbed a sensuous little circle over the back of it before enclosing it in his own broad palm. "Let's go somewhere for dinner where the wine is served in something besides a mason jar and there's not a cowboy steak on the menu. Too many more meals with our friend Ahmed, and I'll be mooing in my sleep!"

"That was very good. I'm surprised."

They were lingering over coffee, the flickering candle adding an aura of intimacy that was abetted by the arrangement of tables in the small French restaurant.

"Oh, ye of little faith." Katherine smiled over the rim of the china demitasse cup. "This is a resort town, you know. It's supposed to have good food."

"Good food, sunshine, and beautiful women."

"What?"

Amber eyes caressed her. "Aren't those the ideal qualifications for a resort?"

"I suppose so," she answered softly, warmed by his gaze. "Hunter, would you like to play tourist tomorrow? I can take you to the botanical gardens or the zoo. Maybe we can even go sailing on Lake Pleasant."

His lips twitched with wry amusement. "Still trying to make a convert out of me, Kate?"

"I just thought that as long as you were staying here, you might as well know what it is you dislike so much."

"I don't dislike it, Kate. Not like you dislike the city."

She expelled a weary sigh, taking her napkin from her lap and placing it on the cleared white damask cloth. "It's no use. You're entirely too closed-minded to accept any new experiences."

"You're wrong about that," Hunter replied easily, rising to take her elbow as they left the restaurant. "But as it turns out, I couldn't tomorrow anyway."

Katherine turned toward him in the dimly lit parking lot. "Couldn't? Are you going to work all day?"

He unlocked the car door, holding it open for her. "No. I promised Monica I'd spend tomorrow with her and Ahmed, watching dress rehearsals."

"Oh," she replied somewhat indistinctly. She slid gracefully into the bucket seat, gathering her full skirt to avoid having the door close on it. "Do you know a great deal about ballet?"

Broad shoulders lifted in a shrug. "Not much."

Hunter closed the door, leaving her alone in the darkness as he went around the front of the car to the driver's side. She'd been thoroughly enjoying herself during dinner. Hunter had related stories about the commodities market that had veered from mind-gripping drama to high comedy.

She'd been spellbound at the enthusiasm in his rugged face and more than once she'd had to stop herself from reaching out and touching the hard line of his jaw as she experienced capricious rushes of tenderness toward him. But now there was a heavy pall over her emotions, and she wondered at the reason.

It had been his offhanded mention of Monica, she realized. And it was this information that suddenly had the answer hitting her like a blow to the head. She was jealous. It was an unpalatable thought, but there was no other explanation. Jealousy, stark and unrestrained, had managed to take control of her heart. As the idea echoed hollowly in her head, she realized the emotion had been building all week.

Katherine and Monica had been friends for so long, and Monica was so flamboyant, that it had been a fairly common occurrence for Katherine to lose a boyfriend to the other woman. Even if Monica herself had done nothing to provoke the incident, Katherine had always seemed to pale, at least in her own estimation, next to her brilliant friend. She'd learned early in life to deal with the experience.

But this time was different. This time her jealousy forked through her like a hot branding iron and Katherine was frightened by the turbulence surging through her. She fully understood, for the first time in her life, those newspaper articles describing crimes of passion.

Katherine rubbed her fingers wearily on the throbbing pulse that was creating a demon of a headache. Hunter, noticing the gesture, patted her thigh lightly, then returned his attention to his driving.

Chapter Nine

"Can I get you some aspirin?"

Katherine was headed directly toward the bedroom when she turned, almost surprised to see him there. She'd been lost in unattractive thoughts about Hunter and Monica's past days together. Those runaway thoughts had created scenarios that weren't easy to take.

"What?" she asked blankly.

"Do you want some aspirin for that headache?"

Katherine shook her head in a negative motion, gritting her teeth at the pain. Full of rocks, that's what her head was, and the movement had sent them all rattling around.

"No, thank you." She turned once again in the direction of her room.

"Hey!" Hunter was beside her in a few long strides. He took her arm and turned her back toward him. "Are you sure you're all right?"

"I'm fine," she lied.

Amber eyes narrowed as he seemed to be making up his mind to say something. "Did I do something to make you angry again?"

"No."

"Uncomfortable?"

"No."

"Then what's the matter, Kate?" His expression was full of honest concern and Katherine tried to tell herself that jealousy was her problem, not his. The demons were in her own mind, certainly. Even if Hunter did have something going with Monica, what business was it of hers?

"Nothing, Hunter," she managed to reply evenly, placing a reassuring hand on his dark-blue blazer. The muscles of his forearm were hard under her fingertips and she longed to touch him further, moving her hand up his arm to his shoulders. She wanted to reach around his neck and feel the short crisp hairs as he gathered her up into his arms.

Crazy. Her mind had turned as capricious as a spring storm and Katherine pulled away as if she'd been hit with a jolt of high-powered electricity. "I'll be fine when I get some sleep," she murmured.

"That's a good idea. I'm sorry about tomorrow," he added, reaching out to stroke her hair gently. His palm followed the silken black waves over her shoulders, roving dangerously toward the soft swell of her breasts. Her breath caught in her throat as every nerve leaned toward his touch. "If I can get away early, want to take that trip to the botanical gardens?"

Hunter's eyes were golden invitations and she realized by the tone of his voice that he was trying to do something nice for her. The man obviously had about as much interest in a prickly-pear cactus as she did in reading the latest in subway graffiti.

"That's very sweet of you, Hunter, but I've got a lot of work to do. I only offered to take you sightseeing because I didn't want you sitting around with nothing to do." It was a blatant lie and Katherine had the feeling Hunter could see right through its flimsy fabric.

"I appreciate the gesture, Kate," he answered simply. "But never fear. Monica has a schedule of appearances booked for K. L. Michaels that would amaze you."

"Monica's always had a lot of energy," Katherine remarked, attempting to rein in the hostility she was feeling at the moment. "I think she could give you a run for your money, Hunter. I can see the two of you now, burning your way through Manhattan."

"She'd fit right in," he agreed, bending to give her a light kiss on the cheek. "Good night, Kate."

Katherine moved into her bedroom, slipping out of the Mexican gauze dress and pulling her Snoopy nightshirt over her head. She washed her face and brushed her teeth, trying to avoid her image in the mirror over the sink. The bleak look in her eyes made them look like two black wells.

Jealous, she rued, throwing the sheets back and climbing into bed. I'm jealous of my best friend over a man I don't even want. To be truthful, she knew that Monica didn't want Hunter either. The one thing both women had in common was that they preferred men they could easily handle, and Hunter St. James was about as easily managed as an uncaged lion. A woman who'd even consider trying to slip a leash on that man was residing in fantasyland, and Monica was astute enough to realize that right away.

So what did it matter? Katherine pillowed her head on her arms, staring up at the bedroom ceiling. What mattered, damn it, was that Hunter and Monica were so much alike, they'd be bound to be drawn to each other. And when faced with the overwhelming masculinity of the man, Monica might be willing to give up a little independence for the promise of sheer rapture. Didn't every woman want to be swept away at least once in her life? And if there was ever a man capable of inducing unconditional surrender, Hunter St. James fit the bill!

She groaned, tossing and turning as she fell into a restless, unsatisfying sleep.

"You're back so early?" Katherine stood in the doorway of the den, shocked to find Hunter back by ten o'clock.

"I got tired of watching those two trade off whip hands," he mumbled, coming into the room.

"What do you mean?"

Hunter shook his dark head, a slanted, wry grin gracing his mouth. "It's really quite a show. For the first couple hours, he struts around with his well-tailored bunch of goons, reminding her none too subtly that it's his money saving her gorgeous neck. Always behind the soft words are the veiled threats that if everything doesn't go exactly as he'd like, he'll pull the plug."

"Poor Monica," she murmured, turning to clean her brush.

"Not *poor* Monica at all." He invested the word with heavy irony. "She, in turn, is flitting about like a brightly hued butterfly, not quite able to decide whether she's going to light on the flower or not. She flirts with him just enough to lead the guy to the brink, then she dances off again. I figure he's gotta be living on cold showers these days. Everytime he hints about taking his money and leaving town, she does her little two-step back a few paces, all sugar and sweet promises." His amber eyes were laughing as he combed long fingers through his hair. "Makes a man weary, just watching that little scene."

"I'm sorry she was too busy playing with her sheikh to fully appreciate you," Katherine blurted out before her mind could censor and halt the outrageously revealing words.

The grooves deepened in his cheeks, as his mouth widened in a slow, triumphant grin. "What's this? Is my Kate suddenly jealous?"

"Of course not," she returned haughtily. "I was just commiserating with you over your failure to compete with the sheikh's vast oil reserves. When faced with such competition, it must be difficult to be just ordinarily rich." She rubbed the brush vigorously, her movements tense and abrupt.

"The only competition I seem to have is this goddamn desert," he said, tucking his thumbs into the soft leather belt as he gazed across the intervening space at her. "And to set the record straight, before that overly active imagination of yours goes spinning totally out of control, I'm not at all interested in Monica. Except to help her out of a jam because she's a nice woman. And your friend. What made you think otherwise?"

Katherine mumbled and turned her back toward him. She hated the look of amusement sparking those tawny eyes. Allowing her feelings to slip out that way had been bad enough, to be wrong about them was humiliating.

"I didn't quite hear that," the deep voice offered.

She spun around, glaring at him. "I said, you both seem to have so much in common."

"I suppose we do. So what?"

"So, it just seemed natural that you'd—well—you'd be attracted to one another."

"You've got it all wrong, honey. What we've got is a basic fact of physics going for us here." He lowered himself into the chair behind the desk, his easy movements showing he'd mastered the contoured furniture. He still didn't look particularly comfortable in it, but neither did he look as if he were in danger of being thrown at any moment.

Katherine waited silently, knowing what was coming and rejecting it ahead of time: likes repel, opposites attract. That was all very nice coming from some textbook, but in real life, it just didn't work.

"I can tell by your face you're already arguing." His tone was low and completely matter-of-fact.

"If you're going to compare it to us, I am," she admitted bravely, meeting his level gaze head on.

"God, she must've made him crazy," he muttered, baffling Katherine, "because I'm rapidly reaching the end of my rope." He lifted serious eyes to hers. "Do you know why I really came back here?"

Katherine noted immediately that Hunter hadn't called it home. It was "back here." This could never be home for him.

"No."

"I came back because I was going crazy not knowing what you were doing. It's as if I'm terrified your life is going to roll smoothly along without me. That I'm not important enough to you to make you think about me constantly, like I do about you. The last five days I've been staying away, hoping that you'll get some sense into that gorgeous head of yours, that you'll realize neither one of us is a complete person without the other."

She watched his trembling fingers as they thrust through dark hair, echoing the ragged tremor of his voice. "Every time that damn sheikh starts raving about K. L. Michaels' painting, I want to rush back here and tell you everything he said. Because I'm hoping that, maybe, just maybe, complimenting your work will get me one smile."

"Hunter, this is all—"

"Melodramatic?" he cut in. "It is, isn't it? Not at all the behavior you'd expect from a button-down stockbroker, is it, Kate? Not even a commodities trader. I know I sound like an idiot. But, dammit, I've told you from the first how I felt. And you won't tell me anything."

His tortured words struck into the very core of her heart and Katherine stared at him, suddenly mute. Before she could say anything, Hunter was out of the chair.

"I think I need to go for a long drive," he said brusquely, "before we find out who's capable of throwing things the farthest around here."

Katherine remained rooted to the spot, aware of the sound of gravel spinning under the wheels as his car pulled away from the house. She watched the billowing cloud of dust disappear and finally found the strength to slump down onto the hard sofa. What if he didn't come back? That was ridiculous. Hunter would never leave without all those clothes he had hung up in the closet of the guest room. Besides, wasn't that what she'd wanted in the first place, for him to go back to New York? So why should this icy hand be gripping her heart?

Because I don't want him to leave, she answered honestly. I love him too much. I want him to learn to be happy here in Arizona, to wear faded jeans and open-necked shirts, and to consider a leisurely stroll in the desert a perfect way to spend a Sunday morning. Hunter St. James, she realized, wasn't the only one who wanted to have his cake and eat it too.

She jumped as the phone rang, answering with a breathless, hopeful note. "Hello, Hunter?" Her face fell into depressed folds. "Oh, hi, Monica. No, Hunter isn't here right now."

She listened to the nearly hysterical feminine tones rising high enough to shatter crystal. "Monica, he just went for a drive. I promise we'll both be there for the performance tonight. Promise." Katherine looked down at her crossed fingers, hoping that she'd be able to deliver Hunter St. James as pledged. She hung up, pacing the room nervously. What did she *really* know about Hunter? She'd never suspected the man had a temper. How did she know he'd be back?

He'll be here, Katherine decided on her umpteenth trip across the flower-strewn tiles. Everything she'd seen had underlined the fact that he was a man of his word. He'd spent the last week jumping in and out of those western clothes, playing out what had to be a difficult charade, because he'd agreed to do it for Katherine and her best friend. He wouldn't let them down now. Not as everything was drawing to a close. The ballet tonight, the rodeo tomorrow, and she'd have her identity back once more. But she wouldn't have the man she'd entrusted it to.

"I realized something while I was out driving around."

Katherine spun toward the deep voice, granting him a warm, sincere, welcoming smile.

"And what was that?"

"I'm glad Daniel didn't win his bid for Spring Snow."

She looked up at him, a quiver of startled reaction racing down her spine. Had she mentioned Daniel St.

James to Hunter when she'd told him the story? Then realization struck. Of course! The name should've brought instant recognition when he'd been so determined to purchase the painting. And while she didn't believe in reincarnation or any other of that mumbo jumbo, all this did smack of a very strange coincidence. Including the almost instantaneous attraction she and Hunter had undeniably shared.

Her eyes widened, dark irises merging with inky pupils as she stared at him and the acknowledgment written on his face.

He moved toward her, cupping her face in his hands, his golden eyes caressing her with stroking touches. "Yes, Kate. I've been waiting for you to make the connection. When you walked into that post office, it was like you'd hit me over the head with a two-by-four. Didn't you feel it, babe? It was as if we weren't strangers at all but something far, far more intimate."

Katherine reached out to trace the line of his full lips. When those lips parted slightly, she slipped a fingertip experimentally inside, feeling a tugging somewhere deep within her as he sucked hungrily.

"Yes," she whispered. "I was afraid, Hunter."

"Don't be, Kate. Don't ever be afraid of me. I won't hurt you."

He reached out, his hands on either side of her waist, pulling her against the warmth of his body. Katherine was overcome with a heady intoxication as his head lowered, his lips tracing the delicate line of her jaw, to tug lightly at her earlobe.

"If Daniel had talked Spring Snow into going back east with him, we'd be related somehow." He groaned with a sudden burst of male desire as Katherine leaned into his body, her arms going up around his neck.

She touched his cheek lightly with her fingertips, turning his lips to hers as she offered him the sweetness within. "Not blood relatives," she whispered against the teasing, probing lips. "She was pregnant with my grandmother before Henri Trudeau abandoned her at the fort. Nothing would've been wrong."

She stood on her toes, lifting herself to the insistent pressure, molding herself against his hard masculinity as a slow, devastating ache spread from her thighs. Her body was rapidly warming to the memory of his lovemaking, every nerve and every pore crying out for the touch of his hands, his lips, the feel of his hard flesh against hers. Her hand moved between them, her palm stroking the growing hardness with loving memory.

"Nothing," he growled deep in his throat, his lips hard as his mouth moved to capture hers. "You're mine, Kate. And it's time you admitted it."

The warmth of his hands as they moved under her T-shirt to play over her flesh created a churning, heated desire within her. Katherine's hands pulled at the snaps on the western shirt he still wore from his morning visit with the sheikh. Then she allowed her fingers to twist in the crisp black hair carpeting his chest. Her hands crept around to his back and she pressed against him, overcome with a need to feel his hard warmth against her trembling body. Hunter shrugged out of his shirt, dropping it to the white tiles, and her celery-green T-shirt followed. Then he bent, placing one strong arm at the back of her knees as he lifted her up, carrying her the short distance to the hard modern sofa. Succumbing to the mystical spell the past was serving to weave around them, neither noticed, nor cared, about the hard surface.

"You'll see," the deep velvety voice promised, "I'll do what Daniel could never do. I'll convince you, Kate, and I'll never give you up. Never!"

"It never would have worked," she gasped as his fingers captured the rosy bud of a nipple, "they were from two different worlds, traveling two separate paths."

"Paths that intersected," he reminded her, his tongue flicking against the erect tip, causing her to writhe under him as her argument rapidly dissolved from her mind.

"Intersected for a time. Then moved apart. In opposite directions," she was able to get out, while twisting her fingers through his dark hair and pressing his head into her yielding softness.

"He promised her everything he was," Hunter replied huskily. "Everything he could be. Apparently it wasn't enough."

"She was already married," Katherine reminded him.

Hunter ceased his wet ravishment of her breasts, pulling his head back to look into her love-softened eyes. He expelled a short, harsh expletive. "To a man who was willing to abandon her at the fort and return to his legitimate wife and three kids as soon as the fur trade dwindled off? How could she profess any loyalty to a man like that? A bigamist. Besides," he said, pounding the hard sofa with his fist to emphasize the point, "there was no way her tribal marriage would've been sanctioned or recognized by the territorial government. She was perfectly free to marry Daniel."

"But Spring Snow considered it sanctioned by a higher power than any government," Katherine argued, firmly springing to the moral and religious defense of her great-grandmother. "And when she begged her father to permit her to marry him, she had no way of knowing Henri Trudeau had another family hidden away in St. Louis. She was only fifteen years old, for heaven's sake, and wildly infatuated with the first foreigner who'd ever shown up at her village. The bottom of the Grand Canyon," Katherine tacked on with emphasis, "wasn't exactly the crossroads of the western world. And Havasu Creek didn't get a lot of people dropping in for a visit."

"Exactly." Hunter leaned over Katherine, hands on either side of her shoulders as he pressed his point. His breath was warm and sweet on her lips as his head lowered treacherously close to hers. "She was only infatuated with the French creep. That's why she should've recognized true love when it was staring her right in the face."

The dark, intense look frightened Katherine momentarily, and for a fleeting instant she fantasized wildly that she wasn't looking up into the face of Hunter St. James. Instead, she saw Daniel St. James as he'd fought to convince Spring Snow to accompany him back to Washington, D.C. She lifted her fingers to ruffle through his crisp waves, combing them into place with gentle, calming strokes.

"Did it ever occur to you, Hunter, that she stayed in Arizona because she loved him so very, very much?"

"A woman's place is with her man, Kate. She should've gone." The deep positive tone allowed no repudiation.

"He wasn't her man."

"Of course he was, damn it! At least in every important sense of the word. They loved each other. Enough that his constant struggle to convince her to marry him cost him his post in Arizona and nearly cost him his career." He put his hand lightly over her mouth, disallowing the point she'd been about to argue.

"They shared everything, Kate. Their hearts, their souls, their bodies. He loved the daughter she'd had by Trudeau like she was his own. Goddammit, Spring Snow was Daniel St. James' woman. And she could never—ever—belong to another man."

Furious amber eyes burned down into her face for a long moment, then Hunter grimaced slightly, as if in self-reproach for physically restraining her. The long fingers released their entrapment of her lips.

"What were you going to say?" he asked dryly, arching an inquisitive but still argumentative brow.

"I was just trying to suggest," Katherine said softly, as if attempting to calm an enraged lion, "that perhaps she was trying to salvage Daniel's career for him. The times were against their relationship succeeding, Hunter. An Indian wife was not a suitable bride for an up-and-coming young cavalry officer."

Her fingers traced the outline of his firmly set lips. "Perhaps she loved him enough to let him go. But you're right about one thing," Katherine added, smiling up into his harsh face.

"I'm relieved you're willing to allow me one point in this little skirmish." Hunter gave her a wry grin. "Just what am I correct about? In *your* opinion?" It was obvious to Katherine that Hunter considered himself unerring on all terms.

"That there could never be another man for her. There never was."

Katherine watched in surprise as Hunter suddenly rolled over onto his back, precariously close to the edge of the sofa. He stared silently at the high ceiling for a time, then turned his dark head in her direction.

"Really? She never took Mary Copperhair and returned to the tribe? I always figured she'd have had to. A young Indian woman alone in those days, with a young daughter to support . . ." His voice drifted off thoughtfully.

"No." Katherine was on firm ground here, no longer having to rely on conjecture. "Spring Snow created a good position for herself by doing laundry and needlework for the women at the fort. There was never another man in her life after Daniel left."

Hunter reached out and drew her against him. "It's a vast relief to know you women remain loyal," he said. "All I have to deal with is that irksome stubbornness you seem to have inherited from Spring Snow. You know, it would've been nice if she'd have been honest as well as independent," he muttered. "Daniel was never really certain she loved him. He was afraid she'd only been responding to a mutual attraction. I don't think he ever really trusted women, after that."

"But he married." Daniel St. James had survived with his hardened male heart intact.

"He married," Hunter agreed reluctantly, as if it weakened his argument. "He'd been assigned as a special officer to the White House. In those circles, it was necessary to do a great deal of entertaining. I think he and Amanda were well-suited. She was a general's daughter who understood the duties of an officer's wife. When his one great romance fizzled out completely, he turned to his work. It was only natural. His big mistake was in allowing Spring Snow to make that crazy decision."

"It was the only way," Katherine murmured, closing her eyes to the erotic sensations stirred in her by the wiry chest hairs rubbing against the tender skin of her breasts.

"I don't believe that, Kate, I never have." The objection rang out in the stillness of the house, a clear, positive sound. "They were fools. Both of them!" Hunter choked, drawing in a deep gulp of air. "Can't you see? It's as if they've been given another chance in us. Let's not make the same mistakes. Don't let it escape us, honey. Oh, God, please!"

The anguished, throaty plea sent a flurry of emotion searing through her body. Was this how it had been for her great-grandmother? When faced with the intensity of Daniel St. James' fiery male need, how could she have ever allowed him to leave? Sent him away, in fact.

Spring Snow, her fevered mind whispered as she arched her body up into Hunter's, I'm not nearly as strong as you were.

Hunter read her silent message instantly. His fingers were lowering the zipper of her white cords when the phone rang. As if of one mind, they both ignored it and Katherine moaned softly, her fingertips digging into his shoulders as he lowered the jeans down her legs.

"Damn!" His lips had been forging a trail back up her bared legs when the incessant phone finally became too irritatingly harsh. "You'd think they'd give up, wouldn't you?"

"Monica," she groaned, her fingers lacing into his hair and tugging him back up to her. "She called while you were gone to remind us about the ballet." Her eyes left his flaming gold gaze and moved to the clock on the wall. "The curtain goes up in thirty minutes."

"Thirty minutes?"

Her own expression mirrored Hunter's disappointment. "Thirty minutes. If we don't go, this charade you've been putting on will all be for nothing."

Katherine watched his tawny eyes blink slowly several times, then a bronze hand moved across his face in a weary, steadying gesture.

"We'd better get ready." His tone was flat.

"I think so," she agreed softly. "Hunter?"

"Yes, Kate?"

"I'm issuing rain checks. Just for tonight if you want one."

His face lit up with all the wattage ever generated by Con Edison. And more. "This is going to be the longest ballet in history," he swore, giving her a hard kiss before moving to answer the still-ringing phone.

"I thought it was very nice . . . for a local production." Katherine chatted lightly as they walked up the brick path to her door.

"Umm. Nice."

"And the sheikh certainly seemed pleased."

"Certainly did." Hunter opened the door.

"Monica asked me to thank you for everything. She's very grateful."

"That's nice."

She looked up at him. "Hunter? Do I have your full attention?"

The flames that burst forth in his eyes told her just how much he'd been thinking about her. Katherine smiled with anticipation, expecting to be carried off to bed once again. But Hunter surprised her as his hands skimmed down her body with an intimate touch and he knelt at her feet.

"Take these silly shoes off," he murmured, lifting her foot into his hand and unbuckling the ankle strap. "I don't know how you women walk in them."

Walk? This was no time for a hike! But she obediently lifted first one foot, then the other, allowing him to slip her shoes off. Katherine stood a good six inches shorter than Hunter, gazing up at him expectantly.

"Now what?"

Hunter clasped his large hand around hers, leading her in the direction of the living room. She cast a backward glance at the couch as he flung open the french doors and brought her outside.

"Hunter? Where are we going?"

"I'd say that's obvious." he murmured, his thumb rubbing sensuous, encouraging circles on the inside of her hand as he continued toward the rolling, moonlit expanse of grass.

Realization struck and she stopped short, digging her heels into the turf. "Hunter, this is a public golf course."

"No, it isn't," he argued, turning back toward her as she balked like a stubborn mule. "It's quite private. I found that out when I had to slip the pro fifty dollars under the counter when I borrowed that club and ball."

"But it's not *mine*, private. It belongs to everyone in the homeowners association!"

"None of whom will be out on the links at this time of night," he stated calmly. "I've had this fantasy since I first saw you Kate. I want to make love to you outdoors. With the stars overhead and your luscious body bathed in moonlight."

"That's crazy, Hunter."

Even as she protested, the idea of lying with him in the soft emerald grass blossomed in her mind. The idea of no constraints, no artificial barriers to inhibit their lovemaking was appealing to her imagination.

No! The idea was crazy. As crazy as Hunter St.

James, and every bit as crazy as the way the man made her feel whenever he merely looked at her. Oh, dear Lord, she was going to do it.

The full moon washed the ground and in its light Hunter could observe the softening of her features. "I promise you," he vowed, kissing her with a tender, almost grateful persuasiveness, "you'll love it. And you'll never forget it."

"Forget it?" She laughed weakly, slipping her hand back into his and allowing him to lead her farther. "How could anyone ever forget making love on the sixteenth hole of a golf course? We'll probably freeze."

"Don't worry, I've every intention of keeping you warm, darling." The throaty insinuation had her blood boiling.

The pristine manicured grounds were a soft plush carpet under her nylon-clad feet as Katherine strolled with Hunter to the foot of a spreading palo verde. The fallen needles had been swept up, the grass freshly mown, and the sweet scent hung in the air like a soft blanket. The entire world about them was lit with a sparkling blue luminosity.

The moon cast shadows from Hunter's long lashes across the sharp planes of his face, and her fingers traced the lines lovingly, tenderly. Her breath caught in her throat at the realization of just how beautiful this man was.

His own gaze lowered from a prolonged study of her uplifted face to the soft swell of her breasts, lightly covered in gold chiffon. His amber gaze hungrily devoured her and Katherine shivered slightly as an aching need clouded her brain.

Long fingers cupped her breasts, massaging the soft curves, and Katherine swayed against him.

"Cold?" he murmured, his eyes possessing enough heat to warm her through an entire season of Arizona winter nights.

"No," she whispered. "In fact, I think I may be in danger of setting fire to this place."

He lowered the zipper and slid the dress off her shoulders to her waist. With a flick of his wrist her filmy bra vanished. His gaze left her breasts, returning to stare greedily into her wide, luminous eyes. Hunter didn't cease the gentle assault of her breasts, capturing each nipple between his thumb and forefinger as he tugged gently, golden eyes watching with satisfaction as her pupils expanded with heightened awareness.

"Do you know what I love?" he asked softly, his eyes holding hers.

"What?" Katherine exhaled delicately, closing her eyes for a long, trembling moment as his stimulating caresses drugged her senses.

"I love the feel of you. And the sight of you. But I especially love the taste of you. You taste like warm sweet summer sunshine. Even at night."

He bent his dark head to taste where his hands had played and Katherine moaned a weak cry as his teeth circled the rosy dark buds of the swelling breasts, tugging lightly but insistently. Her fingers tangled in his crisp hair, and she threw her head back as his seductive lips and teeth and tongue all came into play to send a vibrant need surging through her.

Katherine moved against him in sensuous invitation and felt an overwhelming relief as his fingers lowered her zipper the rest of the way, sliding the chiffon down her hips to fall onto the ground, a golden, moon-spangled puddle at their feet. Now there was only the wispy nylon panty hose keeping those wonderful fingers from etching their flames along her entire length, although a portion of her brain registered surprise they hadn't melted away from sheer, desperate desire.

"Oh, Hunter," she whispered. Her hands captured his and placed them on the soft swell of her hips. "Please, Hunter."

"What do you want, Kate?" His palm was rubbing sensuous circles below her navel, warming her skin through the nylon. "Tell me what you want, darling."

Chapter Ten

"Tell me what you want, darling."

How could she begin to answer that? I want you to love me, Hunter. I want you to love me enough to stay in Arizona with me and I want to love you enough that I can keep you from missing New York. She could have answered with any of those words, but she didn't.

"I want to feel your hands on me." It was reward enough when Hunter took hold of the elastic waistband, slowing lowering the barrier between them. He was on his knees and Katherine cried out into the stillness of the night with a soft, startled cry as his tongue thrust deeply into the slight indentation of her navel.

"Warm," he murmured against her skin as he tasted each exposed bit with his warm, flicking tongue and sensuous lips. "And sweet. Like summer sunshine."

She stepped out of the panty hose, leaning her hips into his roaming lips. Hunter's sharp teeth were taking little bites at the inside of her thigh, and when he'd ravished her skin to the point where she was threatening to explode into a pure, white flame, he moved to her other thigh, purposely avoiding the throbbing, molten core of her.

"Hunter," she sighed, a soft feminine plea.

His hands massaged the softness of her buttocks, his lips hot against her flesh. "Don't worry, Kate. There's plenty of time."

"You're a sadist, Hunter St. James," she gasped as his breath lightly teased against the warmth of her, spiraling her to incredible heights of need she'd never imagined possible.

"No I'm not," he replied huskily, rising to stand over her. His eyes were twin coals in the moon-dappled darkness. "I'm a man who wants to savor every moment of making love to my lady."

He took her hands and placed them on his chest, where she could feel the wild pounding of his heart against her fingertips. It beat in synchronization with the pulsating he'd created within her, a shared, primitive rhythm.

"Undress me, Kate," he said softly, the deep voice thickened with his desire.

Katherine felt as if she were wearing mittens as her fingers refused to obey the commands of her love-drugged brain. But his golden eyes remained encouraging and eventually she was able to shrug the black silk shirt off his wide shoulders.

She could feel the heat emanating from his body and she stood up on her toes, her lips moving lightly against his, her hands massaging the hard muscles of his back. She swayed lightly, a reed in a gentle breeze, brushing her nipples tantalizingly against the firm chest. With an anguished moan, Hunter propelled her into his arms, crushing her full breasts as his mouth suddenly forced passionate warmth between her shocked lips.

"Now who's the sadist?" he growled against her swollen lips. "Get back to work, you erotic tease."

Katherine was stunned once again at just how wonderful this man could make her feel. She felt like a young girl on Christmas morning who'd gotten every present she'd ever dreamed of. She laughed, a deep musical sound.

"You'll have to sit down," she advised him breathlessly. "Those boots are going to be hard."

"Got a lot of experience taking off cowboys' boots, do you?" He twisted his fingers in her hair and Katherine's breath caught in her throat. A dark-indigo cloud moved across the sky, revealing the moon once more. In its silvery glow, she could see the teasing gleam in his eyes.

"No. But there's got to be a reason why they always died with them on. I'd suspect it was because they're tougher than those expensive loafers you're so hung up on."

She was right. Hunter leaned back on his elbows, his legs outstretched in front of him as Katherine knelt between his legs, tugging hard. She managed to pull the first ebony boot off with ease. The second, however, was more difficult, and she tumbled backward, holding it triumphantly in the air as she managed to yank it loose.

With lightning speed, Hunter rolled over on top of her, lightly crushing her into the carpet of thick, fragrant grass, his kiss exquisite and prolonged.

"I think we've just discovered yet another reason why a woman would've been a pleasant traveling companion on the old Chisholm Trail."

"Along with a few others, a bit more basic," she whispered, succumbing rapidly to the heightening intensity of her desire. The feel of his solid frame pressed against her soft contours was like a potent drug and she found she only had a modicum of control left over her shaking limbs. Her pulse quickened and her back left the ground as she arched toward him, needing to feel Hunter's hard male flesh against every inch of her burning, desperate body.

"And I thought we New Yorkers were the ones always in such a hurry," he teased as his body moved sensuously against her urgent pressure. Hunter drank from her moist lips, taking every bit of her breath away. Then he rolled over onto his back, his head pillowed on his arms.

"I believe you were undressing me," he stated calmly, but his amazingly steady voice was betrayed by the rapid rise and fall of the naked, moon-glistened chest.

"A sadist," Katherine groaned, sitting up slowly to give him a mock glare. Her hair tumbled down her bare back like midnight cascading from the heavens as the moon tangled among the thick jet waves to sprinkle the ebony with silver. Her nude body gleamed like pearl and Hunter reached out to touch her as lightly as a breath.

"You are so damn beautiful. I love you, Kate. I never want to wake up another morning without you in my arms."

His love-thickened admission stirred her blood to the boiling point, and though she was far beyond rational thought, a bell rang somewhere in the far reaches of her mind, telling her she'd just received her most heartfelt wish.

"Never again," she echoed. It was all Katherine could do to manipulate the fastener of his pants and pull them down those long, outstretched legs. Her hands feathered lightly back up the strong limbs with intimate, loving touches.

Hunter's head was thrown back onto the grass and

the muscles of his neck stood out in the diffused light. When his eyes opened, they captured hers in a devastatingly hungry look. Katherine thought for a fleeting moment that her heart had stopped.

"Do you have any idea just how much I want you? How much I love you?" Hunter breathed the heated query almost reverently and she nodded, caught in the wild aura he exuded.

"Yes," she whispered. "Because I want and love you. So, so much, my darling." She took his hand and led it down her body, revealing her secrets to him in the most intimate of ways.

"So warm," he breathed as his lips tasted her. "And so sweet. Every inch of you." Hunter was creating sheer havoc with all her senses and Katherine writhed and twisted under his sensual exploration.

"Please, Hunter. Oh, God, please love me."

He settled his weight along her, lifting her gently as he moved between her thighs. His ultimate possession brought waves of tiny shivers skimming through her and her body arched with need into his solid male hips.

"Beautiful," he growled deep in his throat. "You are so beautiful. I love you Kate. I love you."

The words sounded over and over, an incantation that matched the sensual rhythm of their lovemaking. Katherine cried out his name with muffled gasps of pleasure as she felt herself rising higher and higher. Together they were climbing a mountain, the air becoming thinner and thinner as they moved unceasingly toward the summit.

"Hunter. Oh, yes, Hunter. I love you!" Her hoarse pleas for fulfillment became a tremulous cry as they reached the pinnacle together, his name torn from her swollen lips.

Katherine clung to him as if he were a lifeline, preventing her from falling into a dark black crevasse. They shared the slow descent, lying breathless and satiated.

"Oh, Hunter." It was a soft, pleasure-filled sigh.

"And I'd always maintained you couldn't get any real exercise on a golf course." He chuckled, his deep laugh rumbling against her breasts.

"When I first saw you marching across this green, swinging that nine iron with such arrogance, I knew I was in trouble. But I never knew just how much."

His fingers ran up the inside of her thigh, making her wiggle against him with infinite pleasure.

"I think I'm the one in trouble," he said. "I thought the desert was supposed to be warm in the winter."

"It is, comparatively. It's probably snowing in New York right now."

"I'm not this crazy in New York," he alleged, squeezing her. "And it's not exactly scorching out here, darling."

"I'm perfectly warm." Her hands moved up and down his back, stroking his night-cooled skin.

Hunter lifted his head, gazing down into her face with amusement. "Of course you are," he pointed out. "I'm covering you. You're lying there all nice and comfy, stealing all my warmth. While I'm up here, freezing my buns off. Literally."

Katherine heaved an exaggerated sigh. "You should've thought of that before you dragged us out here, Hunter."

He gave her a long, drugging kiss, then rolled off her pliant body to gather up their strewn clothing.

"I only said it was a fantasy of mine," he argued lightly. "In fantasies you don't usually bother to work out all the details."

"You've got a point," she agreed, shivering now that she was deprived of his warmth. Observing the slight tremors, Hunter slipped his shirt around her shoulders.

"Put this on," he instructed, "we'll carry the rest of the stuff into the house."

She laughed. "Do you realize just how ridiculous we'd look if anyone happened by right now?"

Hunter handed her the nylon panty hose and her chiffon dress. "Never laugh at a man when he's naked, Kate. You could cause irreparable damage."

Then, scooping up the last of their clothing, he picked her up, flung her over his shoulder, and carried her back into the warmth of the house.

"Another fantasy?" Katherine arched a delicate black eyebrow as he deposited her lightly on a cushioned stool in the bathroom and began running the water into the high tub.

"It could well be," he agreed, slanting her a seductive grin, "but first thing I've got in mind is to warm up. Then I'm going to work up a nice sudsy lather and wash those grass stains off your lovely back."

The deep voice chuckled as her head swiveled to look over her shoulder and see if he was kidding. "Then, darling, we'll discuss fantasies."

Hunter and Katherine discussed several more enticing fantasies as he moved the terry washcloth over places that could never have gotten grass stains. They also managed to share quite a few before the long night drew to a close. When she finally drifted off into a blissful, contented sleep, Katherine's last thought was that she'd never been so happy.

When she awoke, the smile still curving her lips,

Hunter was no longer lying beside her in the warm bed. But it didn't frighten Katherine. As her mind roused from its sleep, she could remember last night with vivid detail. All of it. Every breathless, ecstatic moment. Hunter loved her and he wanted to spend the rest of his life with her.

She stretched languidly, reaching her arms far above her head, like a lazy, satisfied cat. Katherine Lorene Michaels had everything she could ever want. How had she gotten so lucky?

She shrugged into an emerald-green robe and set off to find him. Habits were hard to change, and Hunter's early rising was just something she'd have to get used to. She located him in the guest room, removing his clothing from the small closet. She'd just opened her mouth to give him a warm greeting when she caught sight of the open suitcase on the bed.

"What are you doing?"

Hunter's rugged features creased into a broad, welcoming smile that at any other time would cause her heart to do a series of small flips. At the moment, however, it seemed to be frozen.

"Good morning, sweetheart. I hope you'll notice I didn't wake you up. I'm getting much better at moving around in the dark."

He slipped a silk shirt off a hanger, folded it meticulously, and put it into the case. "We don't have much time before the rodeo," he continued, moving between closet and bed, "but I thought you'd probably need your sleep. After last night."

Dazed, Katherine stared at him. "Why are you packing, Hunter?"

He picked up another shirt. "To go home, of course. Our little masquerade is over today. There's no more reason to stay."

No more reason? "No more reason?" she repeated aloud. Katherine yanked the shirt from his hands. "What am *I*?" she demanded.

Hunter pulled the shirt from her clawlike fingers, flinging it onto the narrow, single bed. "You're the woman I love." His wide brow furrowed into a puzzled frown. "I thought we'd come to an understanding about that last night."

"Of course we did," she agreed, wide brown eyes encouraging him to continue.

"I don't understand. Is it that you can't get away on such short notice?" Something moved in the depths of his amber eyes. "I figured we'd just take the essentials now and have the rest shipped. Monica will be glad to come pack for you. I'd say she owes us one."

An icy chill washed over Katherine as she belatedly began to understand what he was thinking.

"Hunter, are you suggesting I come to New York with you?"

He, too, began to get the gist of the problem and his tawny eyes narrowed. "Of course."

Katherine stared at him, not liking his arrogant assumption that she'd just pick up and follow him back to that blasted city.

"For how long?" She was willing to put in a few days, or even a couple weeks if that's how long it took. She reluctantly realized that Hunter would have a lot of loose ends to tie up. It would make the time go faster if they were together.

Hunter cleared his throat. "Forever, of course. I was under the impression we'd agreed to make the commitment." Each word was stated separately, punctuated with a low warning.

Katherine licked her lips. "We did. And we agreed to live here."

Hunter squared the broad shoulders, rising to tower over her like an angry Titan. "Here? I sure as hell never said anything about living *here*! My apartment is in Manhattan, Kate."

"And my home is here, Hunter." Her dark eyes gleamed with blatant defiance.

She watched his hands clench into fists at his sides. "Your home is with me, dammit. And that's in New York." He turned back to the suitcase, shoving the shirts in with far less care now. "Are you going to pack," he asked icily, "or shall I do it for you?"

Hunter's uncompromising arrogance sent her temper rising to a slow boil and Katherine inhaled deeply, trying to keep from flinging the suitcase across the room.

"Neither," she said through tightly clenched teeth. "Because I'm not going anywhere, Hunter. I think you've been spending too much time with that sheikh. I'm not some veiled bit of chattel that has to follow obediently three steps behind my master. I'm a liberated American woman with all the rights and privileges that entails."

Hunter's eyes were agates, hard and brittle. "Fine. I don't intend to keep you locked up in the woman's quarters, Kate. So just get ready."

"I've told you, Hunter," Katherine hissed as her hands curled into fists as well, "I'm not going to New York. I'd never be happy living there."

He shook his head in mute frustration. "I could make you happy, Kate. If you'd quit being so damn obstinate, you'd admit it doesn't matter where we live, just so long as we're together."

"All right." She clamped down on the words like a steel-toothed trap. "If it doesn't matter," she dared, "then you stay here with me. And *I'll* make *you* happy."

He came to stand over her, fists balled onto his hips as he used his advantage in height to try to make her back down.

"A woman's place is with her man, Kate," he grated harshly. "And your man's place is in New York."

She sucked in an amazed breath and her eyes flashed killing daggers up, chipping against his dark agate ones. "That is the most old-fashioned, outdated notion I've ever heard of. This is the twentieth century, Hunter! Those chauvinistic attitudes don't wash any longer. It's also the man's responsibility to make adjustments. Why won't you even consider living here?"

"My work is in New York. And I'm getting damn sick and tired of getting up at three in the morning to call London every single day," he shouted down at her.

"So learn some control, Hunter. Would the world come to an end if Hunter St. James missed the opening bell for the London Stock Exchange? Would the entire international monetary system come tumbling down? Would governments collapse if you waited until later in the day?"

He turned back to his packing, refusing to grant her argument a bit of credence. "That's not the point. My work is in New York."

"And my work is here."

"Painting?" His look was honestly incredulous. "You could paint anywhere."

She marched over to the bed, yanking a blue silk tie from his hand to regain his full attention. "I paint cowboys, Hunter," she reminded him with scathing sarcasm. "And as you've already so cleverly pointed out, the only ones you've got in your beloved New York are the rhinestone kind."

His face grew hard and his eyes shuttered, like dark windows. "I'm not going to argue about this, Kate. We've wasted too much time as it is." He reached out and reclaimed the dangling tie from her shaking fingers. "What I'm going to do is finish packing. Then I'm going to that damn rodeo to play out my final scene as K. L. Michaels. *Then* I'm taking a six P.M. flight back home. Home," he emphasized with his fist as it banged into the open suitcase with enough vigor to dislodge several of the ties draped over the top edge. "If you want to come with me, fine. If you don't," he added icily, his wide shoulders shrugging in a dismissing gesture, "it's still your decision. As you said, Kate, you're a liberated lady. Free to make your own choices, even if they are stupid."

Rage rose like bile in her throat at his blatant disdain. Katherine watched, not quite believing what she was seeing as Hunter started in once again with his packing. He ignored her presence as if she weren't even in the room.

"So go back to your precious New York," she yelled, feeling a surge of released retaliation as she slammed the lid of the suitcase down on his hand. "It'll be a relief to get rid of you. I never wanted you here in the first place. I never asked you to come and I certainly didn't ask you to stay. I'm damn sorry I ever painted that stupid portrait in the first place."

Her breasts rose and fell under the emerald satin robe as she breathed heavily, pushing back the thick hair that had fallen over her forehead.

"You're not the only one," he muttered, extracting his hand and flexing the fingers as if testing for broken bones. "And you don't know what a pleasure it'll be for me to get back to women who look like women, not refugees from the Salvation Army mission."

Katherine gasped. "That was a low blow, Hunter." She glared at him, hot traitorous tears stinging her lids. "For your information, the way I dress has always been just fine for here. It's you who always looked out of place. It's you who always *were* out of place."

"You can say that again," Hunter turned his back on her, pulling matched pairs of black dress socks from the drawer. Then he looked at her, his eyes chips of amber ice.

"Face it, Kate. You got caught up in your own damn masquerade. You dressed me up like some fool ranch hand, sent me out to build up an entirely false image of K. L. Michaels, and then you fell for the guy.

"But it wasn't me, Kate. You fell in love with some character who only exists in that overactive imagination of yours. When facing the reality of Hunter St. James in the broad, glaring light of the morning after, it's only natural you'd want to back out of the deal. So"—he shrugged—"you're out. Hell, I'll even give you back *Spring Snow*."

"We made a business deal, Hunter." Katherine gasped at his offer, momentarily shaken out of her anger. "That's the only reason you agreed to the charade. You earned her."

"I don't want her." His voice was cold and flat.

"Well, neither do I. So you've got her," she shrieked, her voice an octave higher.

"She'd only remind me of you," he grated out, slamming the suitcase shut and snapping the latches. "And that's one thing, sweetheart, I don't need."

The cruel words were like a whip lashing her heart and she flinched as he strode past her.

"Go ahead and leave," she flung after him. "And you can bet, Hunter St. James, that I'm going to forget you the minute you walk out that door."

Katherine heard the front door slam with a resounding bang and only then did she throw herself onto the bed and release the torrent of hot, angry tears.

He'd be back, she assured herself later, washing her face in cold water and applying damp compresses to her puffy red lids. It was just a stupid fight. He wouldn't leave it like this.

She applied her makeup with trembling hands, attempting to cover the ravages two hours of anguished crying had etched onto her face. She dressed in the soft gauze dress she knew he liked, put some white wine on ice to chill, and curled up on the hard sofa in the living room for Hunter's return.

The sun set as she waited, but Katherine didn't get up to turn on the lights. She simply sat in the dark, staring toward the front door as if she could make him walk through it by sheer telepathy.

When the bell rang, Katherine raced to the heavy door, flinging it open with a luminous, expectant smile. Her face instantly fell in deep folds.

"Monica."

"We missed you," her friend said, giving her a hug and moving past her into the house. "Why are you sitting around in the dark?"

"Monica, I don't feel up to talking right now. I'm expecting someone."

A penciled brow arched. "Hunter?"

Katherine could only nod, her words were blocked by the lump in her throat.

Monica reached out and put her arm around Katherine's shoulder. "Honey, I put Hunter on a plane three hours ago."

Katherine felt the blood leave her face and her head started spinning.

"Oh, damn," she heard Monica mutter as if from a distance before everything dissolved into a peaceful black void.

"Katherine? Are you okay?"

She opened her eyes slowly, observing the tense expression on Monica's face as she sponged her forehead with a cool damp cloth.

"Did I faint? I never faint," she groaned.

"Mark it down as a first, then," Monica returned. "And it was horribly ungraceful, by the way. Remind me never to do it. You're just lucky we dancers are a lot stronger than we look." Her eyes smiled, encouraging a response, but she didn't receive one. "You're right about this furniture, by the way. It's hard as a rock, but I didn't know if I could drag you all the way into the bedroom."

"This is fine. I don't care," Katherine mumbled, turning her face into the magenta cloth of the sofa.

"That's the same thing Hunter mumbled all afternoon. 'I don't care. I don't care.' Like a broken record. And I think you're both lying." Her emerald eyes gleamed like a cat's in the dim light she'd turned on. "What happened between you two, anyway?"

"I fell in love. Hunter said he did. I don't know."

The terry cloth dipped into the bowl of water as

Monica refreshed it, wringing it out and placing it on Katherine's forehead again.

"Then you dummies have gotten it all wrong. Love's supposed to make you happy. Delirious. Hunter looked as if he were on the way to the guillotine, and you look as if you died sometime last week."

"He assumed I'd take off and go to New York with him. Just like that." Katherine made a half-hearted attempt to snap her fingers, but a dull thud was the only result.

"And you, I suppose, assumed he'd stay here. Like that?"

"Well, why not if he truly loves me?" Brown eyes were threatening to tear again.

"I think he's asking the same question, honey. And I don't think the man's likely to give in."

"Of course not. He's too damn stubborn. He'd rather live alone in his precious, smoggy old New York than share a life here with me."

"You're both fools." The slim woman rose with an incredible amount of grace, considering the position she'd been forced to assume as she'd perched next to Katherine's prone body on the sofa. "I can tell this is not the time to discuss it. I'll be by tomorrow to see if you're in a more reasonable frame of mind." She moved toward the door.

"Monica?"

"Yes, hon?"

"Did Hunter really look that bad?"

"He looked as miserable as I've ever seen a man, Katherine. For the life of me I can't decide which of you looks worse." She shook her flame-tinted hair.

"I'm beginning to feel guilty for even getting you guys together."

"It wasn't you," Katherine muttered, turning her head away from the pity in her friend's eyes. "We got involved a long time ago. Almost a hundred years. It just took us a while to discover it."

"Crazy," the other woman muttered. "Crazy as loons. Both of you. That's the same damn thing Hunter said."

Chapter Eleven

"Is this how you plan to spend the rest of your days?"

Monica leaned back in the comfortable chair, propping her feet up on a crewel-covered footstool, as she eyed Katherine with blatant irritation. Her green eyes were dark and accusing.

"I don't know what you're talking about," Katherine mumbled, long brushstrokes covering the canvas as she allowed her mind a brief flight of fantasy. Hunter appeared this time in the dark-blue garb of the United States Cavalry.

"I mean, you've spent the past six weeks doing nothing but painting Hunter St. James onto enough canvases to fill the Metropolitan Museum of Art. It's getting a little spooky around here. Like a shrine or something."

"That's ridiculous," Katherine murmured, gazing down into the determined amber gaze meeting hers from the oil-covered canvas. She'd come close, but she hadn't quite captured the easy humor of the rugged man. She moved the painting aside, pulling out a new, pristeenly gessoed canvas.

"That's enough, damn it!" Monica was on her feet.

"Katherine, go to the guy. New York isn't so bad. It beats the hell out of a lot of places he could ask you to live in. I imagine that it's our nation's largest city because a great many people enjoy living there. I'll tell you one thing," she said, her tone suddenly deadly serious, "if I ever had a chance to spend the rest of my life with half the man Hunter is, I'd jump at it. Even if he wanted to spend it in Antarctica, sharing an igloo with a bunch of penguins."

"You don't understand, Monica. It's over. There was too much against it."

"The two of you," she complained, going to let herself out, "make a great case for those who believe that insanity is genetic."

Monica left Katherine to her paints and brushes, and it was an exhausted but exhilarated woman who stepped back from the easel twenty hours later. She'd done it! Katherine cocked her dark head, eyeing the painting with red-rimmed bloodshot eyes. At least she thought she had it.

She ran to the phone and made two calls. The first was to Monica. The second was to make a flight reservation at Phoenix's Sky Harbor International Airport.

"It'll be freezing. I brought you a decent coat." Monica shoved the silver-blue mink into Katherine's arms.

"Coat! How can you so casually refer to something that probably cost more than the combined national budgets of half the developing nations, a coat?"

"It is nice, isn't it?" Monica smiled, stroking a sleeve as Katherine tried it on. "I think the color's better on you," the other woman stated without a tinge of envy. "It brings out those deep indigo tones in your hair. Why don't you keep it? Here, it comes with a hat." She placed the Cossack hat onto Katherine's glossy black head, tilting it to a rakish angle. "Perfect!"

"Monica, I can't possibly keep this."

"Of course you can. It's my wedding present. Besides, now that you're going to be living in Manhattan, you'll need it. Probably even find yourself sleeping in it. Remember, those radiators aren't all they're cracked up to be."

Katherine's full wine-dark lips curved with a reminiscent grin. "I don't think I'll be sleeping in it," he said, giving her friend a big hug, "but thanks. I love you. And I'm only going to borrow it."

"You're keeping it," Monica stressed. "Ahmed just came back to town with a refill for his checkbook. I don't need to tell you that the bulk of the reward money should be going to you and Hunter."

"You're a treasure." Katherine squeezed her best friend once more, heading toward the door. "Did you know I was jealous of you for a time?"

"Really?" An auburn brow tilted as Katherine climbed into the passenger seat of Monica's Mercedes, the fur piled onto her lap. "Why?"

"Because of the time you were spending with Hunter."

"Ahmed and I were spending with Hunter. Honey, I didn't have a chance. All that gorgeous man would ever talk about was his terrific fiancée, Katherine St. James. I was beginning to get one helluva complex!"

It was snowing as the cab made its way through the slushy streets to the address Katherine had given the driver.

"I love him." She whispered the words over and over, rubbing the wrapped edges of the painting on the seat beside her like a talisman. "I love him. I really do love him."

Katherine struggled against the claustrophobic feeling imparted by the hulking monoliths lining the street. The shadows cast by the tall buildings turned the afternoon to dusk, shutting out the sun. She tried, for Hunter's sake, to see the skyscrapers not as glass-and-steel fortresses, but as a poetic embodiment of man's universal longing to reach new heights.

"I love him," she reminded herself, her fingers clutching the package.

The driver ignored her mutterings, apparently used to people who talked to themselves in the backseat of his cab.

"I'll have art nearby." She nodded, finding some measure of approval in the towering apartment building that rose directly over the Museum of Modern Art. "Just have to go downstairs. No cowboys, but perhaps it's time for a change."

The battered cab screeched to a halt in front of the building. As Katherine paid the driver, she was suddenly aware of the foolishness of her rash decision. Back in Carefree, surprising Hunter like this had seemed perfect.

But now, with the snow swirling about her in the freezing, wind-chilled air and the deepening dusk, she was no longer so certain. What if she wasn't allowed to wait inside for him? Would she stand out here on the street until she froze to death like Hans Christian Andersen's little match girl? She'd forgotten how cold this place could be in December!

"Hey, lady, you in or out?" The driver growled as she stood poised in the open door of the cab, making her decision. It was suddenly made for her as a second cab pulled up to the curb behind them and Hunter climbed out.

He looked so good! The fur lining on the collar of his overcoat was up around his neck, framing his face. His cheeks were ruddy from the chill, and if his face seemed a little more hollowed at the cheekbones, his eyes were still the lion's gold she'd not been able to strike from her mind.

As if he could feel her intense, loving study, Hunter turned toward her. His eyes widened with disbelief as he saw the elegant, mink-clad woman who was paralyzed where she stood.

"Kate!" Hunter waved toward her as he turned to thrust some bills into the front seat of the cab he'd just left.

"I'm in," she gasped to the driver, slamming the door in her panic. "Take me to La Guardia!"

"Lady, we just came from there, remember?"

"I remember," Katherine shot back, hunkering down into the seat. "And I also remember it's a lucrative trip. So you should be thrilled to do it in reverse."

He muttered something unintelligible under his breath, throwing the cab into gear and pulling out into the stream of traffic. Katherine shut her eyes as she leaned her head back against the seat, unable to dismiss the look of despair that had instantly replaced the one of surprised pleasure on Hunter's face.

Despair washed over Katherine. She should never have followed Hunter.

She was sorry. She really was. He'd looked so perfect here, so New York. And she was so undeniably Arizona. It wouldn't work, and she'd been a fool to think it would. Wishful thinking, that was all it had ever been.

"You in some kinda trouble?"

"Why?" Katherine lifted dull, unhappy eyes to the driver's in the rearview mirror.

" 'Cause we've got that cab tailin' us."

"Lose it," she instructed tersely as her dark head spun around to watch the tailing cab as it wove its way in and out of traffic.

"Look, lady, this ain't the movies, huh? And I'm not Starsky and you're not Hutch. We don't do stuff like that in real life."

Katherine dug into her purse and pulled out some twenties to wave at him.

"Hold on," he instructed brusquely.

Her hands clutched the edges of the vinyl seat as he yanked on the wheel, turning abruptly onto a side street. Her quick glance behind her showed that Hunter's driver had executed the same turn.

For someone who'd always professed to love the peace and quiet of the desert, Katherine was experiencing a thrilling jolt of adrenaline as the two cabs raced through the congested streets of Manhattan, neither one gaining an inch of superiority. She gasped as they jumped a sidewalk and careened around a corner. Katherine shut her eyes, opening them to discover with vast relief that they'd only scattered, and not maimed, the startled pedestrians. A desperate glance in the rearview mirror revealed that while the action had almost given her cardiac arrest, it hadn't done a thing to deter Hunter's pursuit.

She was sliding back and forth, trying to hold onto the painting and her seat at the same time.

"You sure you're not in any trouble with the cops, lady?"

"No," she squeaked as they suddenly swerved. "It's personal."

"Those are the ones that end up getting a guy shot," he muttered, jerking on the wheel. "Hold on, I've got an idea."

Katherine covered her eyes, stifling a scream as they headed the wrong way up a one-way street. The chase was over a moment later, but not because they'd outrun or outfoxed the other driver. It was halted when the cab in the rear plowed into the already well-dented trunk of Katherine's and both cabs came to an abrupt halt.

"Are you all right?" Hunter's expression betrayed his fear as he flung open the door, gathering a shell-shocked Katherine into his arms.

"I am now." A thin note of hysteria edged her voice as she flung her arms around his neck. Snuggling into his embrace, she knew that this was exactly what she'd been missing all these weeks. His beautiful lion eyes caressed her with such loving warmth that Katherine promptly forgot the freezing temperature.

"Are you sure?" Black-gloved fingers moved over her face, like a blind man attempting to memorize her features. "God, Kate, if you'd been hurt I never would've forgiven myself."

His roughened voice echoed the distress visible on his face and she covered his exploring hand with her own. "I'm sure, darling. Are we in trouble?" She looked over her shoulder at the cab drivers, who were engaged in a heated argument.

"I don't know," he answered honestly. "But, if the cops show up, lady, I'm telling them that it's all your fault for running away."

His eyes held a gentle censure and Katherine shook

her head in contrition. "Oh, Hunter, I'm sorry. When I saw you, I panicked. I won't run again, I promise."

"That's good to hear because I can't afford this as a daily habit, Kate. I had to pay that guy forty dollars to take after you."

Katherine laughed, the sound a bit calmer now as she felt safe and secure in his arms. She looked up at him, snowflakes sparkling in her thick black lashes. "I had to pay sixty to get away, but it didn't work."

"It's a damn good thing. As it was, it cost an extra two hundred to convince the guy to use his cab as a battering ram."

"Hunter St. James!" She stared up at him, her mouth dropping open. "Are you telling me that was no accident?"

"Shhh," he whispered against her lips. "Let's let them handle it. There's not three hundred dollars' worth of damage. I think we're going to get off scot-free."

"Not entirely scot-free, Hunter. Because from now on, you're stuck with me."

"I've got something to show you."

Katherine released Hunter reluctantly, allowing him to leave the bed. Her warm brown eyes followed him, drinking in the masculine beauty of the man she loved. Her eyes widened as he tossed a blue-and-white envelope onto the sheets.

"A ticket?"

"One way," Hunter confirmed. "To Phoenix."

"You were coming to me?" Katherine's heart swelled with the knowledge. Hunter loved her just as much as she loved him. She hadn't been wrong to come to New York.

"I was. To ask you to become Katherine St. James

for real. You should be used to the name by now," he teased lightly, "and I was bringing your ancestor back to Arizona. So she'd feel at home."

They both looked up to where the portrait of Spring Snow hung, the wall space now shared by a likeness of a vibrantly masculine, amber-eyed cavalry officer.

"Is that how you see him?"

Katherine welcomed him back under the blankets, snuggling in against his hard body. "I don't know," she answered honestly. "I don't know if it's how I see Daniel. Or you. Sometimes you both get mixed up in my mind like a dream."

Hunter laughed, a deep, rumbling sound she felt against her breasts as he pulled her nearer, his hands running down her bare back.

"I know the feeling, sweetheart, but we're a lot smarter than they were. I've been thinking about it. I could probably use a few months every so often to unwind and learn how to appreciate all the beauty Arizona has to offer." His desirous gaze included her in the natural wonders of her state.

Her lips brushed his lightly. "You know, I really do love the museums. And the theaters. The restaurants are very nice, too." She kissed the corners of his lips.

"I'll deed over my den for your studio," he pledged. "It gets a lot of light, being up this high. And if it isn't enough, we'll buy the penthouse on the top floor and cut a hole in the roof."

Katherine laughed softly, her hands tracing little patterns in the crisp hair covering his chest.

"And everything's waiting for you back home. Arizona home," she corrected, knowing that wherever

Hunter St. James was, that was where her home would be.

His hands had been making a warm exploration down her sides, but now they stopped as he gave her a crooked, questioning grin.

"You kept the ticker-tape machine?"

"I did." She nodded. "It's been running the entire time you've been away. I didn't have the heart to turn it off," she confessed softly. A sudden gleam shimmered in her eyes, momentarily revealing the pain she'd suffered. "It was as if by letting it clatter away, you'd walk in the door any minute."

His palm stroked her long hair, his expression shadowed with shared grief as he lifted his eyes back up to the painting of Spring Snow. "I know," he murmured. Then, shaking his head as if to dispel any sad times they might ever have to experience again, he raised dark eyebrows. "What have you done with all that ticker tape?"

"I saved it."

"For what?"

Katherine laughed, a full, satisfied sound as she rolled over on top of him, one hand reaching out to pull the sheets over their heads.

"I'm going to have a parade. Our very own private, welcome-Hunter-home-again ticker-tape parade."

"Oh, Kate," he growled as his lips tasted hers with a sweet urgency. "You've already done that in grand style. Now it's my turn to welcome you."

Katherine surrendered to Hunter's devastating caresses, knowing that with homecomings such as this, any spot on earth would be nothing short of heaven.

TELL US YOUR OPINIONS AND RECEIVE A FREE COPY OF THE RAPTURE NEWSLETTER.

Thank you for filling out our questionnaire. Your response to the following questions will help us to bring you more and better books. In appreciation of your help we will send you a free copy of the Rapture Newsletter.

1. Book Title: _____

   Book #: _____ (5-7)

2. Using the scale below how would you rate this book on the following features? Please write in one rating from 0-10 for each feature in the spaces provided. Ignore bracketed numbers.

   (Poor) 0 1 2 3 4 5 6 7 8 9 10 (Excellent)
   0-10 Rating

   Overall Opinion of Book................ _____ (8)
   Plot/Story............................. _____ (9)
   Setting/Location...................... _____ (10)
   Writing Style......................... _____ (11)
   Dialogue.............................. _____ (12)
   Love Scenes........................... _____ (13)
   Character Development:
   Heroine:.............................. _____ (14)
   Hero:................................. _____ (15)
   Romantic Scene on Front Cover......... _____ (16)
   Back Cover Story Outline.............. _____ (17)
   First Page Excerpts................... _____ (18)

3. What is your: Education: Age: _____ (20-22)

   High School   (   )1   4 Yrs. College (   )3
   2 Yrs. College (   )2   Post Grad   (   )4 (23)

4. Print Name: _____

   Address: _____

   City: _____ State: _____ Zip: _____

   Phone # (   ) _____ (25)

Thank you for your time and effort. Please send to New American Library, Rapture Romance Research Department, 1633 Broadway, New York, NY 10019.

RAPTURE ROMANCE

Provocative and sensual, passionate and tender— the magic and mystery of love in all its many guises

Coming next month

PASSION'S PROMISE by Sharon Wagner. When her long-ago first love Ben Cumberland reentered her life, Joyce Cole felt all her defenses crumbling. But would the passion he promised cost her the independence she'd worked so long to achieve. . . ?

SILK AND STEEL by Kathryn Kent. Though their wills clashed by day, at night Ryan and Laura were joined in sweet ecstasy. But did the successful promoter really love the young fashion designer—or was he only using her talents to settle an old business score?

ELUSIVE PARADISE by Eleanor Frost. For Anne and Jeremy, a private business relationship turned into an emotional, passionate affair—that was soon the focus of a magazine article. Then Anne began to wonder if Jeremy was interested in her, or publicity for their business venture . . .

RED SKY AT NIGHT by Ellie Winslow. Could Nat Langley fulfill trucker Kay O'Hara's every dream? Nat had designed the rig she'd always wanted, and Kay had to find out whether he was trying to sell himself—or his truck—to her . . .

BITTERSWEET TEMPTATION by Jillian Roth. Chase Kincaid haunted Julie King's thoughts long after he'd broken her heart. Now he was back, reawakening dreams and desires, making her fear she'd be hurt again . . .

RECKLESS DESIRE by Nelle Russell. Novelist Justin Reynolds was the most magnetic male Margot Abbott had ever met. But what kind of love story were his caresses creating for Margot, who knew him so little yet wanted him so much. . . ?

GET SIX RAPTURE ROMANCES EVERY MONTH FOR THE PRICE OF FIVE.

Subscribe to Rapture Romance and every month you'll get six new books for the price of five. That's an $11.70 value for just $9.75. We're so sure you'll love them, we'll give you 10 days to look them over at home. Then you can keep all six and pay for only five, or return the books and owe nothing.

To start you off, we'll send you four books absolutely FREE. "Apache Tears," "Love's Gilded Mask," "O'Hara's Woman," and "Love So Fearful." The total value of all four books is $7.80, but they're yours *free* even if you never buy another book.

So order Rapture Romances today. And prepare to meet a different breed of man.

YOUR FIRST 4 BOOKS ARE FREE! JUST PHONE 1-800-228-1888*

(Or mail the coupon below)
*In Nebraska call 1-800-642-8788

Rapture Romance, P.O. Box 996, Greens Farms, CT 06436

Please send me the 4 Rapture Romances described in this ad FREE and without obligation. Unless you hear from me after I receive them, send me 6 NEW Rapture Romances to preview each month. I understand that you will bill me for only 5 of them at $1.95 each (a total of $9.75) with no shipping, handling or other charges. I always get one book FREE every month. There is no minimum number of books I must buy, and I can cancel at any time. The first 4 FREE books are mine to keep even if I never buy another book.

Name	(please print)
Address	City
State Zip	Signature (if under 18, parent or guardian must sign)

ℛℛ *Rapture Romance*

This offer, limited to one per household and not valid to present subscribers, expires June 30, 1984. Prices subject to change. Specific titles subject to availability. Allow a minimum of 4 weeks for delivery.

RR 183

RAPTURE ROMANCE

*Provocative and sensual,
passionate and tender—
the magic and mystery of love
in all its many guises
New Titles Available Now*

(0451)

- **#45 ☐ SEPTEMBER SONG by Lisa Moore.** Swearing her career came first, Lauren Rose faced the challenge of her life in Mark Landrill's arms, for she had to choose between the work she thrived on—and a passion that left her both fulfilled and enslaved... (126303—$1.95)*
- **#46 ☐ A MOUNTAIN MAN by Megan Ashe.** For Kelly March, Josh Munroe's beloved mountain world was a haven where she could prove her independence. but Josh—who tormented her with desire—resented the intrusion. Could Kelly prove she was worth his love—and, if she did, would she lose all she'd fought to achieve? (126319—$1.95)*
- **#47 ☐ THE KNAVE OF HEARTS by Estelle Edwards.** Brilliant young lawyer Kate Sewell had no defense against carefree riverboat gambler Hal Lewis. But could Kate risk her career—even for the ecstasy his love promised? (126327—$1.95)*
- **#48 ☐ BEYOND ALL STARS by Melinda McKenzie.** For astronaut Ann Lafton, working with Commander Ed Saber brought emotional chaos that jeopardized their NASA shuttle mission. But Ann couldn't stop dreaming that this sensuous lover would fly her to the stars... (126335—$1.95)*
- **#49 ☐ DREAMLOVER by JoAnn Robb.** Painter K.L. Michaels needed Hunter St. James to pull off a daring masquerade, but she didn't count on losing her relaxed lifestyle as their wild love affair unfolded. Could their nights of sensual fireworks make up for their daily battles? (126343—$1.95)*
- **#50 ☐ A LOVE SO FRESH by Marilyn Davids.** Loving Ben Heron was everything Anna Markham needed. But she considered marriage a trap, and Ben, too, had been burned before. Passion drew them together, but was their rapture enough to overcome the obstacles they faced? (126351—$1.95)*

*Price is $2.25 in Canada

To order, use the convenient coupon on the next page.

RAPTURE ROMANCE

*Provocative and sensual,
passionate and tender—
the magic and mystery of love
in all its many guises*

			(0451)
#33	☐	APACHE TEARS by Marianne Clark.	(125525—$1.95)*
#34	☐	AGAINST ALL ODDS by Leslie Morgan.	(125533—$1.95)*
#35	☐	UNTAMED DESIRE by Kasey Adams.	(125541—$1.95)*
#36	☐	LOVE'S GILDED MASK by Francine Shore.	(125568—$1.95)*
#37	☐	O'HARA'S WOMAN by Katherine Ransom.	(125576—$1.95)*
#38	☐	HEART ON TRIAL by Tricia Graves.	(125584—$1.95)*
#39	☐	A DISTANT LIGHT by Ellie Winslow.	(126041—$1.95)*
#40	☐	PASSIONATE ENTERPRISE by Charlotte Wisely.	(126068—$1.95)
#41	☐	TORRENT OF LOVE by Marianna Essex.	(126076—$1.95)
#42	☐	LOVE'S JOURNEY HOME by Bree Thomas.	(126084—$1.95)
#43	☐	AMBER DREAMS by Diana Morgan.	(126092—$1.95)
#44	☐	WINTER FLAME by Deborah Benét.	(126106—$1.95)

*Price is $2.25 in Canada

**Buy them at your local
bookstore or use coupon
on next page for ordering.**

RAPTURE ROMANCE

*Provocative and sensual,
passionate and tender—
the magic and mystery of love
in all its many guises*

(0451)
- #19 ☐ CHANGE OF HEART by Joan Wolf. (124421—$1.95)*
- #20 ☐ EMERALD DREAMS by Diana Morgan. (124448—$1.95)*
- #21 ☐ MOONSLIDE by Estelle Edwards. (124456—$1.95)*
- #22 ☐ THE GOLDEN MAIDEN by Francine Shore. (124464—$1.95)*
- #23 ☐ MIDNIGHT EYES by Deborah Benét (124766—$1.95)*
- #24 ☐ DANCE OF DESIRE by Elizabeth Allison. (124774—$1.95)*
- #25 ☐ PAINTED SECRETS by Ellie Winslow. (124782—$1.95)*
- #26 ☐ STRANGERS WHO LOVE by Sharon Wagner. (124790—$1.95)*
- #27 ☐ FROSTFIRE by Jennifer Dale. (125061—$1.95)*
- #28 ☐ PRECIOUS POSSESSION by Kathryn Kent. (125088—$1.95)*
- #29 ☐ STARDUST AND DIAMONDS by JoAnn Robb. (125096—$1.95)*
- #30 ☐ HEART'S VICTORY by Laurel Chandler. (125118—$1.95)*
- #31 ☐ A SHARED LOVE by Elisa Stone. (125126—$1.95)*
- #32 ☐ FORBIDDEN JOY by Nina Coombs. (125134—$1.95)*

*Prices $2.25 in Canada

Buy them at your local bookstore or use this convenient coupon for ordering.
THE NEW AMERICAN LIBRARY, INC.,
P.O. Box 999, Bergenfield, New Jersey 07621
Please send me the books I have checked above. I am enclosing $_____
(please add $1.00 to this order to cover postage and handling). Send check or money order—no cash or C.O.D.'s. Prices and numbers are subject to change without notice.

Name_____

Address_____

City _____ State _____ Zip Code _____

Allow 4-6 weeks for delivery.
This offer is subject to withdrawal without notice.

REBATE COUPON

SPECIAL $1.00 REBATE OFFER WHEN YOU BUY FOUR RAPTURE ROMANCES

To receive your cash refund, send:

1. This coupon: To qualify for the $1.00 refund, this coupon, completed with your name and address, must be used. (Certificate may not be reproduced)

2. Proof of purchase: Print, on the reverse side of this coupon, the *title* of the books, the *numbers* of the books (on the upper right hand of the front cover preceding the price), and the U.P.C. numbers (on the back covers) on your next four purchases.

3. Cash register receipts, with prices circled to:
   Rapture Romance $1.00 Refund Offer
   P.O. Box NB037
   El Paso, Texas 79977

Offer good only in the U.S. and Canada. Limit one refund/response per household for any group of four Rapture Romance titles. Void where prohibited, taxed or restricted. Allow 6–8 weeks for delivery. Offer expires March 31, 1984.

NAME_____

ADDRESS_____

CITY_____STATE_____ZIP_____

SPECIAL $1.00 REBATE OFFER
WHEN YOU BUY
FOUR RAPTURE ROMANCES

See complete details on reverse

1. Book Title _____

   Book Number 451-_____

   U.P.C. Number 7116200195-_____

2. Book Title _____

   Book Number 451-_____

   U.P.C. Number 7116200195-_____

3. Book Title _____

   Book Number 451-_____

   U.P.C. Number 7116200195-_____

4. Book Title _____

   Book Number 451-_____

   U.P.C. Number 7116200195-_____